ChangelingPress.com

Trucker/Vicious Duet
A Bones MC Romance
Marteeka Karland

Trucker/Vicious Duet
A Bones MC Romance
Marteeka Karland

All rights reserved.
Copyright ©2021 Marteeka Karland

ISBN: 9798733181486

Publisher:
Changeling Press LLC
315 N. Centre St.
Martinsburg, WV 25404
ChangelingPress.com

Printed in the U.S.A.

Editor: Katriena Knights
Cover Artist: Marteeka Karland

The individual stories in this anthology have been previously released in E-Book format.

No part of this publication may be reproduced or shared by any electronic or mechanical means, including but not limited to reprinting, photocopying, or digital reproduction, without prior written permission from Changeling Press LLC.

This book contains sexually explicit scenes and adult language which some may find offensive and which is not appropriate for a young audience. Changeling Press books are for sale to adults, only, as defined by the laws of the country in which you made your purchase.

Table of Contents

Trucker (Bones MC 6) 4
   Chapter One 5
   Chapter Two 17
   Chapter Three 33
   Chapter Four 44
   Chapter Five 57
   Chapter Six 70
   Chapter Seven 79
   Chapter Eight 90
Vicious (Salvation's Bane MC 1) 102
   Chapter One 103
   Chapter Two 115
   Chapter Three 126
   Chapter Four 137
   Chapter Five 152
   Chapter Six 166
   Chapter Seven 184
   Chapter Eight 193
   Chapter Nine 210
Marteeka Karland 223
Changeling Press E-Books 224

Trucker (Bones MC 6)

Marteeka Karland

Helen -- I've made some bad choices in my life. The worst was falling for a man who kidnapped me and held me hostage. He wants my baby. Why, I have no idea, but there's no way he's getting it without a fight. Once this is over, assuming I'm still alive, I'm going to need some serious help.

Trucker -- The small redhead blows me away at first sight. And not only because of the knife sticking out of her very pregnant belly. She's fierce as a tiger. Brave as any member of Bones. I know I have to protect her, no matter what kind of trouble she's in. Once she's healed, I know she's going to be mine. I just have to convince her of it. Until then, I'll protect her, and her kid, with my very life. Once the asshole who did this is dead, then I'll prove to her why I'm the best choice to be her man.

Chapter One

"Trucker! You pussy! Where's the fuckin' cage?"

Trucker rolled his eyes and sighed. "Right where you fuckin' left it, you bastard!" He had no idea who was calling out, but it didn't much matter to Trucker. It was all pretty much the same every time a member of the club needed a vehicle other than their own bike. He'd long ago given up being really angry. Besides, it was all part of the camaraderie.

"Ain't you in charge of all the vehicles around here?"

"Yep. Ain't no Goddamned babysitter though. And I ain't your Goddamned housekeeper! You take somethin', you can damned well put it back where you found it."

"Fucker!"

Trucker continued working on the bike in his shop, a grin tugging at his lips. The men of Bones could act like kids sometimes. It was all part of the fun. They'd had several close calls recently, and the whole of Bones needed to have a little fun.

That was the beauty of Bones. They'd started out as an MC club of men. Now, they were becoming a family complete with wives and children. Trucker was gratified to see Cain and Torpedo encouraging the change. Oh, they still sometimes skirted the edge of legality and wouldn't hesitate to do what had to be done to protect their own people, but now they did more toward protecting their community. Their reputation was mostly enough to keep out the rabble who thought they'd just run roughshod through Somerset. The ones who weren't as afraid as they should be soon learned to be.

Thirty minutes later, Torpedo, their vice president, came into his shop. "Seriously, Trucker. Where's the fuckin' RV?"

Trucker didn't look up from his task. "In the barn where I intend to service it when I get done servicing the bikes in here."

"Not that RV, the other one."

He looked up. "The '80 Winnebago?"

"Yeah. Couple of the prospects wanted to go huntin'. I told them they could take that one. Figured if they trashed it, you wouldn't have to kill them over it."

Trucker snorted but went back to work. "You know better. They take it out, they bring it back like they found it. With everything clean. Including the fuckin' toilet."

"Not a problem. Except, we can't find it."

"It's in the other bay in the barn. Serviced it for Cheetah a couple weeks ago. She always puts things back where they belong. Must be the absence of the Y chromosome."

"Cheetah?"

Trucker paused, looking up at Torpedo. "Yeah. Said she needed it. Didn't see no reason not to let her have it. Didn't think she was gonna be out this long, but ain't none of my business. And I know I saw her just a few days ago."

"Hmm. Well, it's gone."

Trucker shrugged. "Give her a call. See what she's got goin' on. She called first dibs though. Ain't tellin' her she's got to come back, and neither are you or any of the others."

"Hey. I had no intention. She may not be a patched member, but she's done good by the club and ExFil."

"Text her. Make sure she actually has it. I'd hate to have to start the fuckin' day with a killin' if that fucker Pig took it."

"I thought Stunner took care of that little fuck?"

"He did. Boy seems to have responded to brute force more than all the fuckin' talkin' and smacks upside the head in the world."

"Good thing Mama was able to patch him up. I was worried about the fucker for a while there."

Trucker shrugged. "He'd been asking for it for a while. Guess him mouthin' off to little Suzie wasn't the worst thing he did, but maybe it will be the last."

"Boy can't even look at Stunner without shivering." Torpedo laughed. "It's funny as shit."

"He got what he deserved. I just hope he learns from it."

"Sent a text. Though, I don't remember seeing Cheetah today. She's probably got the thing parked at some community event. Wasn't there a fun run today? She usually makes hot chocolate and coffee, or lemonade and iced tea for things like that."

"Good point." Trucker took out his phone and sent off a quick text to Cheetah behind Torpedo's before shoving it back in his pocket. She might ignore one text for a few minutes, but not two.

"Bikes look good?" Torpedo nodded to the line of six bikes Trucker was servicing.

"Yep. Routine stuff." Trucker pointed to Torpedo's bike. "You could go a little easier on the brakes."

Torpedo grinned at him. "Now, what fun would that be?"

"No fun if you end up on the pavement."

"True that."

Torpedo turned to go, but Trucker called to him. "Let me know when you find Cheetah and my RV." He didn't have to wait long. Trucker actually heard the old Winnebago long before he saw the thing.

Picking up a rag to wipe off the wrench he was using, Trucker walked outside his workshop into the brisk, February air. Off in the distance, *screaming* up the long driveway to the clubhouse, was the missing RV.

"What the everlasting fuck? Torpedo!"

"I see it, Trucker." Torpedo was just outside the building talking with Bohannon, Sword, and Viper.

"Is that Cheetah?"

"Don't know. Comin' in hot though."

"Look out!"

The Winnebago made a sharp turn and slid to a halt next to the clubhouse in the parking lot. Several men jumped out of the way. A few seconds later, the door to the back flew open. Cheetah stumbled out.

"We need Mama! Help!"

The men headed for the RV. Bohannon yelled for Luna, his woman, to go for Mama and Pops. Trucker ran for the RV along with the others. Something made him... uncomfortable. There was a tingle between his shoulder blades that always meant there was something wrong. What it could possibly be, Trucker couldn't imagine. Not in their home territory. Cheetah had brought the RV into their clubhouse, so he doubted she'd brought danger to their door.

An ear-piercing shriek came from inside the Winnebago. A woman? The men looked at each other before Bohannon, who was closest, shoved Cheetah out of the way and entered the vehicle. Trucker was right behind him. What he saw froze his blood.

There was a table that folded down into a bed across from the stove and counter. On that bed lay a very pregnant woman who had been stabbed in the abdomen. He knew she'd been stabbed because the knife handle was still sticking out. The blade appeared to have been stabilized, probably by Cheetah, but the wound was steadily and persistently dripping blood onto the thin mattress and down to the floor.

Sweat beaded the young woman's face, strands of dark auburn hair sticking to her forehead and cheeks. Her expression was one of pain, fear, and grief. Her gaze locked with Trucker's, sea-green eyes sparkling like diamonds with her tears. "Help me. Please." Her voice was tremulous. Her lips quivered as tears coursed from her eyes down her temples.

"What the fuck happened here?" Bohannon demanded as he checked the small area for anyone else.

"What's it look like?" Cheetah bit out. "She's been fucking stabbed! Get her to Mama!"

Trucker couldn't seem to move. He was caught in some kind of web as he continued to stare into the young woman's eyes. He couldn't register much other than the brilliant green of her eyes and the red blood staining her clothing around the knife.

"Get her inside," Bohannon ordered. "Luna's gettin' Mama, but she can't do anything out here. Not enough room."

When Bohannon moved to the girl, Trucker shouldered his way in front of his brother, carefully scooping her up into his arms. Her hands were covered in blood, one shaking horribly where it fluttered close to the knife. He could tell she wanted it out but knew better than to just yank.

"Easy," he said, as he turned sideways to get them out of the small door. With his size and her advanced pregnancy, they barely fit, and he had to be careful not to jar her too much with that knife stuck in her abdomen. "Just relax if you can. We'll get you taken care of."

"No police," she gasped.

Trucker looked up sharply at Cheetah as he got them on firm ground, out of the RV. She just shook her head before falling into step behind them. Later. He'd deal with that later. Getting the girl to Mama was the main concern at the moment.

"They call me Trucker," he said as he strode up to the clubhouse in long, confident strides. "What's your name, little miss?"

"Helen."

"That's a good name." He smiled down at her as he turned the corner into the clinic Mama had set up for the club. "Fittin' for such a beautiful girl."

Fuck. Now he sounded like a putz. A quick glance up had Pops and Mama both raising their eyebrows. Bohannon walked into his line of vision, and Trucker noticed the enforcer had a similar look of amusement on his face. His eyes said he'd be laughing his ass off if the situation were any different.

"Is there anyone we need to call for you, Helen?" Pops asked, his voice that soft, soothing tone he had when the situation called for it.

"No. Nobody." Helen looked to Cheetah, who nodded.

"Bohannon, I think you need to take Cheetah outside. She has something to tell you and Cain." For Pops to call out Cheetah so obviously told everyone how unhappy he was with the woman.

Helen's eyes widened in panic and she tried to sit up, but a firm hand on her shoulder by both Mama and Trucker stayed her.

"Trust us, girl," Mama said gently. "You're protected here."

Helen looked to Trucker much like she'd looked at Cheetah. A query as to whether everything would be all right. "I've got your back, Helen," he said. "No one's gonna hurt you while you're here."

That seemed to be what she was looking for because Helen laid her head back on the table. Her gaze clung to Trucker's though. For some reason, she'd latched on to him even more than she had to Cheetah. The girl had glanced at the door once as the other woman left, but had kept her attention focused on Trucker after that.

Mama moved around her, cleaning around the wound to check for continued bleeding before bringing in an ultrasound machine and running it over Helen's belly.

"How do you have this stuff?" Helen's voice was soft and so filled with pain it made Trucker wince.

"Mama and Pops are special, talented people. Bones has the means, so we make sure they have what they need to take care of all of us."

"Just relax, dear. I need to see what the knife hit and what needs to happen next." Mama moved her hands gently over the girl as she spoke.

"I don't want to go to the hospital," she said immediately.

Mama kept working, seeming to ignore Helen. Pops moved to stand next to Trucker, laying a gentle hand on Helen's head. "We may not be able to prevent it, young lady," Pops confessed. "We don't want to risk harming the baby any further."

At the mention of her unborn child, Helen's hands slid to her abdomen. She caressed the uninjured side and barely stopped herself from doing the same to the side with the knife buried deep.

"I know, but if he finds me, he'll finish what he started." Her voice broke on the last and she bit her lip, closing her eyes tightly as tears leaked steadily.

"Who did this, honey?" Papa asked gently. "Tell me so we can make sure he never does anything like this again."

She shook her head violently. "*NO*! I told Carol. She was getting me out, but he found out anyway and look what happened!" Helen was panicking. Mama had hooked up monitors to her before beginning her exam with the ultrasound, and Helen's heartbeat was wild.

"Carol." Trucker raised an eyebrow. "You mean Cheetah?" Trucker doubted many in Bones knew that woman's real name. If anyone did. He sure hadn't known her name was Carol. That this girl did meant she was important to Cheetah in some way.

Helen looked confused. "Carol. She brought me here."

Trucker nodded, sitting beside Helen in a nearby chair. She automatically reached out for his hand, grasping it in a death grip. Without thinking, he covered her small hand with his other large one. For long moments, Trucker just stared at their entwined hands. All he could think was how different they were. She was this small, fragile woman while he was a large warrior. It was up to him to slay her demons.

And why the fuck was he thinking like this? He didn't know this lady and didn't owe her anything. But he knew in his heart he absolutely would protect this small woman to the death if necessary.

"Good news is," Mama began, never taking her eyes from the screen as she made adjustments and measurements to the image the ultrasound provided her, "the baby appears unharmed." She fiddled with a few things, pressing a few buttons as she adjusted the probe on Helen's stomach. "Bad news is, the child won't stay that way long. You're losing amniotic fluid." She looked at Helen, a serious but determined look on her face. "How far along are you?"

"A-about nine months, I suppose. Best I can count."

"You suppose. Have you had any prenatal care?"

Helen's gaze slid away, ashamed. "Not since I was sixteen weeks. He wouldn't let me, and I couldn't keep up with the days because he sedated me sometimes."

"You're gonna tell me who this fucker is, Helen. Them I'm gonna kill the sumbitch," Trucker growled before he could stop himself.

She glanced at him sharply, fear in those lovely eyes.

"Not now, Trucker," Mama chastised in an impatient voice. "There are more important things to worry about right now. Pops, I'm going to need some resources. You know what to do."

"I'll be right back." He patted Helen's head gently before leaving the room.

"First thing we've got to do is start a couple of IVs. This isn't going to be easy or painless, but I promise you we'll be quick and careful. I'll also make sure you have as much medicine as I can safely give you before we start. If all goes well, your pain will be minimal. Mild discomfort at most."

"What's going to happen?" Helen's hand tightened around Trucker's as she looked from him to Mama. "Can you help me and not hurt my baby?"

"I'm going to try," Mama said. "Should be pretty straightforward. You're very lucky the knife missed both the baby and anything vital to you. Once we deliver the baby and make very sure you're not bleeding internally from someplace I can't see with the ultrasound, you both should be fine. We just have to be careful. Pops is getting some help for me."

"He's not calling the police, is he? I can't have the police involved." She looked terrified at the mere thought.

"Honey, this is Bones. We take care of our own, and we do it on our own."

"Carol said that too."

"Then believe in that. We'll take care of you." Mama smiled gently as she set up several instruments and sealed packs on a nearby table. When Pops came back in, he did so with an isolette for the baby when it was born, and a warmer, which was essentially a big heat lamp though more precisely controlled.

Helen's eyes got big when she saw the equipment, but before she could say anything a pain hit her. Must have been excruciating because her scream was even louder and more intense than it had been when Cheetah had first opened the door to the RV. After one sharp scream, she pressed her lips tightly together and squeezed her eyes shut.

Mama was there, with the ultrasound, concentrating on the side of her belly beside where the knife had penetrated before moving the probe to different angles around the knife.

"It's cutting you with each contraction," Mama muttered. "Slicing muscle and letting more fluid escape."

"Help's on the way," Pops said to her softly.

Ten minutes later, Mama had monitors hooked up to Helen, IVs started, and all kinds of medical equipment ready. Even though Trucker had seen the woman work on members of Bones and their families before, it always amazed him how much equipment and supplies she managed to have hoarded away out of sight. She also had a wealth of people with important skills in the community who owed her favors.

A man entered from the back room. He wouldn't have had to go through the common room, but had been admitted from the back by Pops, his identity preserved as much as possible. "Mama, I swear, if I pull this off, we're even."

Mama chuckled. "Maybe. But you'll still help if I call you. If for no other reason than you have a need inside you to help people in trouble."

The two talked at length, carefully planning out what they would do. When Helen became distressed, Trucker tried to distract her. Thankfully, there wasn't another contraction like the last one. Trucker wasn't certain he could take the anguished sound of her scream, knowing she must feel like she was being sliced apart from the inside out.

"You're in good hands, you know. Mama is the best there is."

"Who is she?" Helen's voice shook and her hand tightened around Trucker's again, but she seemed to be holding up.

Trucker shrugged. "One of us. We don't ask too many questions when someone wants to keep their private life private. We just do our best to help out where we can."

"So, if I wanted to keep my past a secret, you'd let me? Once this is all over, I can just leave?"

"We'll talk about that later." Trucker didn't want to sound hypocritical, but he didn't want to lie to her either. "Just get through this. Get the baby here. Everything else will take care of itself."

Chapter Two

Helen woke to a sharp pain in her abdomen. The smell of antiseptic was astringent but oddly soothing. She hadn't been in a clean room in longer than she could remember. Not clean like this. Sure, she'd kept her room clutter free and as clean of dust and dirt as she could, but she hadn't been allowed any chemicals or anything that might harm the baby. She'd longed to really deep clean her surroundings, especially over the last few weeks, as she knew the time neared for her to have her baby.

Absently, her hand moved to her abdomen. She froze. There was no movement inside her. Her belly wasn't nearly as big as it had been.

"Noooo!" The cry was torn from her. Had Levi actually done it? He'd told her he'd take her baby the second it was born and there was nothing she could do about it. "My baby!"

"Shh, shh, shh... hush now." The voice was gravelly and gruff but gentle. She remembered that voice from before. Trucker? Was that his name? "Everything's all right. You're safe."

"My baby. Where's my baby?"

"Over there in the bassinette." He gently turned her head to the side so she could see the clear-walled bed the infant slept in peacefully. "She's fine. Mama checked her out thoroughly. Not a scratch on her. Little small, but seems otherwise healthy."

Her gaze snapped to Trucker's. "A girl?"

"That's right. Little girl. The women are out shopping for the little princess as we speak. By the time you're ready for visitors, they'll have the nursery painted, decorated, and ready for you to move her in. Data's already got baby monitors all over the fuckin' clubhouse, and if I see another pink stuffed animal, I'm making every single member of Bones turn in their man cards."

At any other time in her life, she'd have laughed. Given everything that had happened to her over the past year, she couldn't find it in her.

She looked down at her torso. A hospital gown covered her, but she easily moved it aside to examine her belly.

"Mama says you're fine. She says you'll need to heal for several weeks before you can leave here."

"What about…" Helen wasn't sure she wanted to bring it up, but she had to know. "Can I still have children if I want more?"

"Can't answer that, baby. You can talk to Mama when she checks on you later."

"How long have I been out?"

He shrugged. "Twenty-four hours. You woke up fine after the surgery, but Mama thought it best to keep you out for a while to let your body heal."

"Who's been taking care of my baby?"

"Mama. Cheetah and some of the other women took a turn too. Especially Angel. She's expecting, herself, and was excited to help." He smiled at her. "You'll have all the help you need until you're feeling better."

"No one's going to take my baby, are they?"

"Honey, anyone tries, they gotta go through me. Don't worry about that. Worry about getting better so you can spend some quality time with the little lady over there."

Helen winced as she tried to move. Pain sliced through her, sharp and wicked, an uncomfortable reminder of what had happened the last time she'd trusted a man. Which brought everything back in sharp relief.

"Did you guys call the cops?"

"Why are you so against the cops helpin' out? Looks like they need to get some thug off the street."

"No cops," she said firmly. "It will make things exponentially worse."

Trucker nodded slowly, obviously not liking her answer. "OK then. No cops. You gonna tell me what's going on?"

"You told me Bones didn't mind if people kept their secrets. This is mine."

"I can't help you much if I don't know the situation."

"It's not your problem. I'll be fine."

"Oh, really?" He leaned back in his chair and crossed his arms over his chest. Which was when Helen began to realize just how big this guy was. She might be more in over her head than she'd been before she escaped Levi, and that was saying something. "Didn't look like you were fine when I found you."

That made her stomach roil. Just the thought of everything that had happened made her ill with panic. Levi had caught her when Carol had tried to get her out of that hellhole. He'd told her he was going to cut the baby out of her, and he nearly had. If Carol hadn't come back for her…

Without warning, her stomach heaved. Helen didn't have much in her stomach, but what little she did came out in an explosive gush. Vomit and bile seemed to be everywhere. On the bed. On her. In her hair. On the floor. Over and over, she heaved. Trucker helped her lean over the side of the bed and held her hair out of her face. Helen was sure he'd gotten sprayed at some point, but he didn't acknowledge it or react in any way.

"What on Earth?" Mama hurried into the room. She got towels and a basin, tossing both to Trucker. "What happened?"

"I said something I shouldn't have, and her body reacted."

Helen lost track of the conversation then as she fought for control. Her abdomen hurt like hell, and she was afraid she'd torn something loose. With great, gasping breaths, she finally stopped heaving. She still felt sick, but the nausea was passing with every second.

"Lie still, child," Mama said gently. "Let me get some clean bedding and a shirt for you. We'll get this fixed up."

"I need to go to the bathroom," she said, her voice wavering pitifully.

"I got you." Trucker started to help her out of bed, but Helen had had enough. She couldn't go head-to-head with this man right now. She just wasn't up to it.

"No! Just... I can do this myself." Helen pushed at him weakly, but managed to get to her feet on her own.

"I'll be right here if you need help," Mama said. "Be careful you don't hurt yourself." The older woman glared at Trucker, and her tone changed drastically. "You. Out." It was a command. Nothing less. Surprisingly, Trucker said nothing. He only nodded before following her orders. Helen wondered if it was respect that had such an obviously Alpha male following orders from the woman. She thought it might be. Trucker was a bit rough around the edges, but he'd shown her and everyone around him respect from the moment she met him. Didn't mean she was going to let him take over her life. From this point on, Helen was determined she would be responsible for own happiness. Not a man, or anyone else.

In the bathroom, she relieved herself, careful not to move too quickly. Her abdomen hurt badly, but she found it was manageable if she just went slowly. Once done, she patted her face down with water. There were dark circles under her eyes, and her face was thin. Undoubtedly she'd lost a lot of blood and was probably still a bit dehydrated. Helen looked around, found a toothbrush still in the package, and helped herself. She found a robe hanging behind the door and, again, helped herself. It was quite a bit too large for her, but she put it on anyway. It was either that or leave the bathroom naked. She'd puked on everything else.

Before putting on the robe, she examined her belly. Where the knife had been was a stitched area. Below that, another stitched wound she could only presume was from a C-section. She'd have some nice scars, no doubt. Small price to pay for her life and the life of her child.

Helen opened the door tentatively, fully expecting Trucker to be standing just outside waiting on her. But he wasn't in the room. Mama was just finishing making the bed, but no one else was there.

"Feel better, child?" She smiled warmly at Helen. Helen liked Mama. She wasn't sure she was ready to trust her, but she thought she might get there.

"Where's Carol?"

"Cheetah? She's having a talk with Cain, the president of Bones."

"About me?"

Mama raised an eyebrow. "No. I think they intended to talk about painting Cain's Harley a nice shade of pink." She crossed her arms over her chest. "Good topic of conversation, huh?"

"That your way of saying, 'duh'?"

"It's my way of saying you need to learn your surroundings. Yes. They're talking about you. I doubt there is another topic of conversation anywhere in the clubhouse right now, and I'm pretty sure you know that. These people aren't your enemies, Helen. They want to help, and they want to protect you and your daughter."

Helen slumped against the wall, tired beyond anything she could ever remember. The months she'd spent with Levi had grown increasingly terrifying, but she hadn't really done anything other than sit in the basement room where he'd locked her. After the stress of the fight to escape, the attack on her, then running for her life, not to mention whatever surgery these people had done to her, Helen's body and mind were completely worn out.

"I haven't had time to process everything." She placed her hands over her abdomen as she'd done a thousand times over the last few months. Not feeling the child inside her gave her a panicked feeling. Like her baby was no longer safe. Fighting the sensation was proving difficult. Now that the nausea had passed and she was better in control of herself, not to mention starting to get a handle on the whole situation, there was only one thing she truly wanted. "I need to see my baby." Helen tried to sound strong, like she was, indeed, feeling better. Instead, she knew she sounded as fragile as she felt.

"Of course," Mama said, reaching out a hand to Helen and leading her to the bassinette. In the little bed lay the smallest, most beautiful baby Helen had ever seen. Her breath caught, and tears filled her eyes. She reached for the sleeping child and gathered her into her arms.

Awe filled her, and an overwhelming sense of urgency. She needed to get scarce. Someplace Levi could never find her. They hadn't even left the city. It was only a matter of time before he came looking for her. Carol had managed to hurt him, but he wasn't dead.

"You're sure she wasn't hurt? She's well?"

"I'm positive. She's a bit small, but since you weren't exactly sure when your due date was, it may just be she was premature. But she seems to be doing fine. She's eating small amounts and has wet diapers. My guess is that in a few days, she'll be eating like a horse and demanding your full attention."

"I asked before, but Trucker said I should ask you." Helen looked up from her child to face Mama, needing to look into the other woman's eyes when she asked her next question. "Will I be able to have more children?"

Mama smiled. "You will probably need to have a C-section, but you should be able to have more children. It would be a high-risk pregnancy and need to be monitored very closely, though."

That rubbed Helen the wrong way. She felt like Mama was chastising her for not getting adequate prenatal care, though it wasn't her fault she hadn't. "You know, you have no idea what I've been through. I don't mean to seem ungrateful, but I'd planned on being monitored closely during this pregnancy. Circumstances beyond my control prevented it." The moment the words left her mouth, Helen was ashamed of herself. Mama wasn't accusing her of anything.

Simply answering Helen's question as completely as she could.

Instead of going on the defensive, the other woman gave a satisfied smile. "You'll be fine. And fit in here quite nicely, I might add. All I meant was your injury was traumatic to your uterus. As it stretches and expands to accommodate another child, it risks leaking fluid or rupture. No one is judging you for things beyond your control, dear."

"Who was the man you had helping? Will he go to the police?"

"He's an old friend. And no. He won't go to the police."

They sat in silence for a while after that. Helen looked down at her sleeping child. A little girl. She had a daughter. "I'm responsible for this whole little person," she murmured. The gravity of the situation hit her pretty hard. She'd been stabbed, then given birth under extreme circumstances with people who seemed to have means and resources they shouldn't. She'd definitely brought this child into the world under questionable conditions.

"Yes, dear. You're responsible for this tiny little thing. She will exhaust you, try your patience, and frustrate you to no end. But she will be the most important person in your life and your greatest accomplishment." Mama placed a hand on her back and rubbed gently. "She's lovely, Helen."

Helen looked up at Mama. "How long do I need to stay put before it's safe to travel?"

Mama looked at her, tilting her head in disapproval. "If I were you, I'd give it at least a couple of weeks. You're going to be very uncomfortable for a while and, should you overdo it, there's still a very real chance you could hemorrhage."

"I see." Helen studiously avoided looking at the other woman, cuddling her baby to cover her discomfort.

"You know, you could stay here. In fact, I'd highly recommend it until they find the bastard who did this to you."

She smiled up at Mama briefly before continuing to look at her child. "I appreciate that, but I don't want to be more of a burden than I've already been. I need to get moving as soon as possible." Mama was silent for a while, but Helen could feel her disapproval. "I'm really sorry," Helen finally said to break the tension. "It's not that I don't trust you. Hell, we probably wouldn't be here if it weren't for all of you. But I don't know you or what you are or how you have all this equipment or know doctors who are willing to come into a place like this and assist with a birth after the mother's been stabbed and still not go to the police." Her words ran together in her haste. She had no wish to offend anyone, but she was scared as hell to stay in Somerset.

"Bones is... complicated. I promise you this is the safest place you could possibly be. But you need to consider telling us everything. This group can work miracles if you just give them enough time."

* * *

Trucker waited outside the clinic area where Mama had kicked him out. He wasn't letting Helen far out of his sight until he established some kind of rapport with her. Besides, just being away from her, knowing she needed someone to be there for her when he couldn't be, was a decidedly uncomfortable feeling.

Fuck uncomfortable. It sucked ass.

"How's the little mama doin'?" Torpedo approached from the great room.

"Understandably distraught. But hanging in."

Torpedo looked at the door, then back at Trucker. "Why are you out here instead of in there? You've been by her side every fuckin' second since she got out of surgery."

"Fucked up."

Torpedo gave an exasperated sigh. "Already? Fuck, Trucker."

"Hey. I never half-done anything in my life. Why start now?" He tried to sound flippant about it but he'd never felt more like a failure.

"You guys need to go to some sensitivity training or some shit. Learn how to not piss off your women."

"Oh, yeah? Wait till you get yourself one. See how fuckin' easy it is. Besides. She's not my woman."

"Yet."

"Whatever." Trucker crossed his arms over his chest and stood guard in front of the door where Helen was currently recovering. He wondered how long he should wait until he tried to get back in. To distract himself he took the opportunity to question his vice president.

"What did you find out from Cheetah?"

Torpedo's gaze snapped to Trucker's, anger flashing there. "It's bad, brother. She did the right thing by getting Helen out of there when she did, but she should have gotten us for backup." He scrubbed a hand through his hair and down his face. "Girl was being held captive by this guy named Levi Redding. Apparently he targeted her for the baby."

"Huh?"

"We've been checking into this guy, Trucker. He provides babies to desperate couples. For a price. His goal with Helen was to sell the baby. From what Data found, every time he does this, the mothers are killed after the child is born. I have no idea how many kids he's sold off or how many women he's killed, but it sounds like he moves around a lot. Probably from one moderate-to-small town to another."

"A fucking serial killer?"

"And a black-market baby factory."

Trucker felt like someone had punched him in the gut. "Cain gettin' a team together to go rip this guy's nuts off?"

"You know it, brother. Sword, Bohannon, and Shadow are doin' some recon. Once we know what we're going into, we'll shut those motherfuckers down."

"What the fuck?" Rage simmered close to the surface inside Trucker. "How did Cheetah get involved in this?"

"It's a miracle she was, Trucker. She just happened to know Helen, or the girl'd be dead right now. Missed her a few months ago and started lookin' for her. Went for her soon as she found her. Apparently she cut it fuckin' close. Bastard was fixing to --"

"I get the picture, Torpedo! What the fuck?"

"Hey. You asked."

"Yeah. I did." He bumped his head against the wall a couple of times, trying to process everything Torpedo had told him.

"Tell me what you're thinking, Trucker." Of all his brothers in Bones, Torpedo probably knew him the best. Hell, Torpedo was vice president for a reason. Cain knew their capabilities and unique skills intimately. He also knew how far he could push them, when to push them, and when to back off. Torpedo could read their emotional states and was able to balance his knowledge with Cain's. Right now,

Torpedo could probably tell how confused and upset Trucker was when he was normally solid.

Trucker took a deep breath. "Torpedo, there's a woman in there I can't seem to let go of. I saw that knife sticking out of her belly and looked into her eyes and knew I'd do anything in the fuckin' world to protect her. She don't know me, and she's under a tremendous amount of stress, but my mind and heart are tellin' me she's fuckin' mine. I can't seem to back off."

Torpedo shrugged. "Show her why she should accept you. Then protect her and her child with your Goddamned life."

That must have been all Trucker needed to hear, because he took a deep breath and his mind seemed to center. Things had just become simple. He had one job. Protect Helen and her baby, and she'd accept him. He knew because of the way her gaze had clung to him earlier. Before he'd acted like an ass. She trusted him. Probably because he was a big son of a bitch.

Just in time, too, because Mama opened the door to her clinic and stepped out. "Trucker. You're still here?" She raised an eyebrow. "I thought you be somewhere kicking puppies."

He winced. "That's harsh, Mama."

"So's upsetting that girl so much she becomes physically ill. You should be ashamed of yourself."

"Believe me, Mama. I am." He nodded toward the interior of the clinic. "Helen all right?"

"No. But she's better." Mama looked him up and down. "If you're looking to make a better impression, I suggest you mind your manners this time. That girl needs a rock in her life. Not a boulder smashing down on top of her."

"Understood. Can I go in?"

"You're a good man, Trucker. Normally, I'd tell you to go to hell. Helen has been through more than any woman should have to endure. It's only because I happen to believe she needs you that I'll make an exception. I saw the way she looked at you. She believes you're the best person to keep her safe. Probably because you're fucking big."

Trucker grinned. "I had that exact same thought."

"Then get on with you," Mama said, an exasperated look on her face. "But this is it, Trucker. No more second chances."

He wasn't giving her time to change her mind. Trucker nodded once then entered the room, shutting the door behind him.

* * *

Was there anything as soothing as holding a sleeping baby? Helen didn't think so. Mama had given her some comfortable pajamas that didn't aggravate the surgical incision or the wound on her abdomen where she and the other doctor had delivered her baby and repaired the damage done by the knife. Now she sat in a rocking chair, surrounded by pillows and rocking the baby girl she'd yet to name. Her mind was just... overloaded? Was that the right word? She couldn't think. Not about anything. So she sat there, rocking her daughter and humming softly.

The door to the clinic opened and Trucker stepped inside. His gaze found her immediately and seemed to hold her captive. Like a coward, Helen broke his stare by nuzzling the baby in her arms.

She should have known he wouldn't stay away. He was the kind of man who was persistent, not letting something go until you kicked him in the balls. She could tell that by the way he'd shouldered his way around the other man who'd entered the RV to get to her side. He'd done his best to soothe her and had stayed with her. He'd even been the first person she'd seen when she woke up. Mama had said he hadn't left her side during anything. He'd changed into scrubs and done everything Mama had told him to in order to stay with her. She'd been a staunch advocate for the big man, and Helen had to wonder why.

When he entered the room and looked at her, her breath had caught. One of the reasons she'd had to get away from those all-seeing eyes. She wasn't sure if she were sexually attracted to him because she wasn't ready to think about stuff like that, but she certainly loved to look at him.

He had the look of a man who could get things done. Brawny and rugged, he wasn't a man whose capabilities you had to question. She could well believe he was capable of anything he wanted to do. He was big. Like *hella* big. Muscles bulged from his arms, and veins roped the length from his biceps to his hands. Thick, chestnut-colored hair grew past his collar and was just messy enough to make him look like a woman had been steadily running her fingers through it. The color matched his beard, which was thick but cut neatly in contrast to his hair. Dark brown eyes seemed to glitter at her as he looked her over from head to toe. But it was his hands that fascinated her. They were large, but lean. They looked like they were skillful with small things. Dexterous.

"Hey there," he said by way of greeting. "How you doing?"

Helen tucked a curl behind her ear. "Good. Mama said I need a few weeks of rest then I'll be out of your club's hair."

He tilted his head, his eyes narrowing. "Who said you were *in* our hair? We're glad you're here. Cheetah did the right thing bringing you to us."

"I'm glad she did. I just don't want to be a bother. You have to know I bring a lot of baggage with me."

"Doesn't everybody?" He stalked toward her. It was the only way she could think to describe the way he moved. When he knelt down in front of her, he took one of her hands in his big, rough ones. "We're looking into the situation. Cheetah told us she suspected he targeted you because you were pregnant. We're pretty sure he's a serial killer and sells babies on the black market. If that's the case, he moves from place to place. We're going to find him and take care of the situation. Until then, I'd hope you'll trust us to make sure you and your daughter are safe and taken care of."

God, she wanted to believe him! She almost could when he was gentle like this. But she'd seen his ruthless side. Just a peek, but it was there. "I appreciate it, Trucker. Really. But once Mama says I'm OK to leave, I intend to. I want as far away from Somerset as I can possibly get."

He sighed, obviously disappointed. "If that's your wish, none of us will stop you. You're going to be here for a while anyway. Why not think about it? Get to know the women and let them help while you're here. You may find having a big family like this is just what you need right now."

She hadn't thought about it like that. "I thought this was a motorcycle club."

"We are. But we're also a paramilitary organization and a family. All the men have served together in one capacity or another. Some for ten years or better. We're all part of ExFil. That's Cain's company. The women are here for various reasons. Some of them, like Cheetah, have military experience of their own."

"Cheetah. You mean Carol?"

"Yeah. Not sure any of us knew her real name before you came along. Well, other than Cain, and he don't spill stuff like that."

"She's been my best friend since we were five," Helen said softly. She remembered the wonderful times they'd had, the trouble they'd gotten into. All of it. "If she hadn't missed me…"

"But she did. And she brought you to us. If you don't trust me, trust Cheetah. Can you do that?"

"Of course."

"Good. We'll get you settled in a room with an extra bedroom you can use as a nursery. You'll have privacy and space, as well as someone close by if you need help."

She found herself nodding even though she didn't really think it was a good idea. If she entrenched herself here, she'd never want to leave. Regardless of what she'd been through with Levi, she *did* feel safe here. More, she felt herself latching on to Trucker. She'd been in his company for less than an hour that she remembered, but she could feel herself reaching out to him and his strength. If anyone could keep her safe from Levi, it was Trucker.

"Good. Now." He grinned at her. The effect was devastating. She was in so much trouble. "Introduce me to the little one here."

Chapter Three

The morning of her eighth day at the Bones clubhouse, Helen awoke in her room alone for the first time. Up until today, every time she'd woken from a nap or a night's sleep, Trucker had been there, lazily dozing on the couch. She'd found him more than once changing the baby and making baby talk with the girl, which Helen thought was uproarious. The child had cooed and gurgled, not paying him much attention past the bottle or the dry diaper. Now, Helen was alone. No note. No telling her he was outta here before he left. Nothing. She was surprised at how much it hurt.

There was a knock at her door, and she just knew it was Trucker. She hurried to open it and found Carol there with a big smile and a hot breakfast.

"Hey, girl. Glad to see you on your feet this morning." It was the first time Helen had been out of bed for more than a few minutes at a time since she'd awoken from her ordeal. Carol had been to see her every day.

"Are you going to tell me what's going on today?" It was a point of contention between them. Helen knew Bones was planning something, but refused to tell her what. Instead, she just changed the subject. Her favorite topic?

"Have you thought of a name for the baby yet? You can't keep calling her Bunny, Honey Bunny, and Sugar Plum forever."

Helen sighed, more disappointed that she was ready to admit. "No. I'll think of something soon, I'm sure."

"Well, if you can't figure something out, you might keep Carol in mind. That's a good name."

"Better than Cheetah?" She asked the question while looking her friend in the eye. She was grateful beyond measure for the other woman's interference, but this was a whole other world her best friend was involved in. And Carol had never said a fucking word.

"Ouch." Carol winced. "I guess I deserved that."

"I thought I knew you. You certainly knew me. This is off the charts, Carol!"

"I know. But it's just not something I talk about. I'm here with Bones because I'm an employee with ExFil. This is a way to de-stress and be around people who know what it's like to be in a combat situation. This feels more like a home than I ever had with my folks."

Helen didn't know what to say to that. She sighed. No reason to hang on to resentment. Helen was a bit of a goody two-shoes in that department. She'd never had so much as a speeding ticket. Ultimately, it was more important to have Carol's friendship that it was to have been in the loop on this. "I'm glad you found a place you belong, Carol. And thanks for coming after me."

"Couldn't let my best girl disappear on me." She tried for a bright smile, but the tension was just too much. "I'm really sorry I didn't tell you about this, Helen. I just didn't know how you'd react to me being involved in a motorcycle club."

"So, tell me about it now. Are you a member?"

"No, not as such. They haven't started patching women yet, but I think Cain's considering it because of me. He's mentioned it several times, just hasn't taken the plunge yet."

"Wow. Sounds kinda chauvinistic."

"Not really. At least, not this club. They treat me like a patched member in some cases. They let me in on meetings and even ask my opinion on occasion. It's just not official, and I don't get a vote."

"What about the other women here? Are they like you?"

"Naw. Most are patch chasers. Women who want to be with a patched member either as a steady lay or an ol' lady. Some just like the atmosphere and the partying. There are currently five ol' ladies in Bones. Cain's wife, Angel. Bohannon's woman, Luna. Storm and Magenta are a couple as well as Viper and Darcy and Arkham and Rain."

"Are they good people? MCs have a certain reputation. I hope you haven't fallen in with the same kind of situation I was stupid enough to get involved in." Helen was more than a little ashamed she'd gotten herself into such a mess, but there was nothing for it now.

"They're really good people, Helen. Give them a chance, and I think you'll love them."

"You're not usually up here this time of day. Something going on?"

Carol looked at the tray of food she'd set on the table. "Why not come eat? Pops fixed pancakes just for you. Said you wolfed them down yesterday."

Avoiding her question again. "Fine," she said softly. In Carol's defense, the pancakes were awesome. They were worthy to be a distraction, but Helen resented her friend not being straightforward with her. Instead of trying to carry the conversation, Helen just ate in silence. Carol seemed content to do so as well. Which was just for the best. Helen saw the anxious looks her friend was giving her between bites. No doubt, whatever was going on had something to do with her and the baby.

She cleared her throat. "You know, if Trucker is with another woman, it's fine with me. It's not like we're an item or anything. I know he's been here a lot, but I've got more important things to worry about, and I'm sure he does, too. You don't have to be uncomfortable around me because of him."

"No, Helen! Trucker isn't with another woman. It's got nothing to do with that."

"Then it's me. Did I get you in trouble with your club when you dragged me home? I'm sure I'm a mess they didn't need."

Carol grabbed her hand. "You listen to me, honey. Right now, nothing is more important to this whole club than you and this baby, and Angel and her baby. Everyone is circling the wagons to keep the two of you safe while they hunt for Levi."

"You think Angel is in danger from Levi? Oh, my God!" Helen was horrified. It was bad enough she'd caused so much trouble already, but to think she might have put an innocent woman in the same position she'd been in made her want to vomit.

"God, no! Are you kidding? These men would crush any trouble headed Angel's way! Hell, so would I! I'm just saying they consider you just as important as Angel. And that's saying a lot. Angel is Cain's ol' lady. If you weren't already aware, Cain is the president. His interests are always put first with the club."

She wanted to question Carol further, but there was a knock at the door followed almost immediately by the door opening. Trucker stepped through it with several bags.

"I come bearing gifts," he said with a smile. Then his gaze landed on Helen's. Immediately, it shifted to Carol, a thunderous look coming over him. The man was seriously protective. "What the fuck'd you do to upset her?"

Carol raised her hands. "Wasn't me, bro. You don't want your woman upset? I suggest you don't leave without telling her where you're going." She grinned before leaning in to give Helen a hug. "I'll see you later. Mama says you still need rest. Make sure you get it."

She nodded faintly, but her gaze was glued to Trucker. God, he was sexy! And *big*. She doubted she'd ever met a larger man. Probably her hormones giving her a workout, but just that intense look he got sometimes was enough to send her libido into overdrive.

When Carol was gone, Trucker sighed. "I'm sorry," he said, looking very contrite. "I shoulda told you I was leavin'."

"No. You shouldn't have." She shrugged. "It's not like we're a couple. You don't owe me anything. If one of us owes someone, it's me."

"Then what's got that worried look on your face, little mama?" He was gentle as he raised a hand to brush her cheek gently before tucking a curl behind her ear.

"You guys are doing something that involves me. I don't want anyone hurt because of it."

"Believe me, honey. No one's gonna get hurt. Especially not because of you. But we *are* hunting that son of a bitch Levi Redding. We can't leave him loose in our territory. Too many people at risk."

"What have you found out?"

"You sure you want to know? I won't lie to you, but you need to make sure you're ready to hear more about this guy. You need to heal, and you have a new baby to take care of and bond with. I don't want you stressed."

"I'm sure. I need to know."

Trucker sighed, but nodded as if expecting her answer. "Data's back-trackin' him over several states. Everywhere he goes there's a pattern of missing pregnant women. Some turn up. Others not. So far, we've not found any evidence any of the babies have died, so he's had some practice."

"Oh, God," she whispered, her hand reflexively going to her abdomen where she'd been stabbed. Where her baby had rested until a week ago. "How many times has he done this?"

"We don't know yet, but I'm guessin'... several. Enough that there's a trail to follow. Data's on him. Tracked his movements over three years and continuing. So far, he's found five different aliases."

"What about here? In Somerset? Did he move after Carol rescued me?"

"Oh, yeah. But Data's got him pinpointed. Carol was smart. She managed to get a tracking pellet on his person."

"She fought him off me," Helen said, nodding.

"It's not a foolproof way to keep track of him, but so far, we're in luck. She got it in his jacket pocket so he's kept it with him and not washed it yet. Right now, it looks like he's hiding out in a rural part of the county, still near Somerset but out of the way. We can see him moving around, going for supplies, things like that. Probably waiting to see if there is backlash from your escape. He'll give it another couple of days. When there's no police response, he'll probably pack up and move out. To do that, he'll need a different car. He may shuck his identity before he leaves. It would be the smart thing. Data has feelers out with two of the best identity forgers in the area. If they hear anything, they'll let us know."

"Wow. Sounds like you guys are pretty well connected."

He shrugged. "Sometimes, we need to do things off the radar and outside the realm of legality. Suffice it to say it pays to know people in the underground."

She ducked her head, trying not to look as uncomfortable as she felt. She'd never been one to do much she wasn't supposed to do. Hell, she didn't even litter. This man was *submersed* in doing things he wasn't supposed to do. She wasn't judging, just… what was she supposed to say?

"How did you end up with this Levi character? I can't imagine you went willingly."

"Well, you'd be wrong." She gave him a faint smile. "I met him about four months ago. I was sixteen weeks pregnant at the time -- another round of poor judgment on my part and a story for another time. We dated for a couple months, then I got kicked out of my apartment out of the blue. Something about renovations on my unit. It never really made sense, but the guy wanted me out. Levi just happened to be with me when it happened and offered a place to live. The second he had me inside his house, I was a prisoner. He locked me in the basement. He only came in to feed me, make sure I took my prenatal vitamins, and let me know that if I didn't carry the baby to term, he'd kill me. Now I understand he'd planned on killing me anyway." She hung her head. "Should have figured that one out sooner, but I wanted to believe he'd let me go. Kinda stupid, but there it is."

"You're not stupid, Helen. It's normal to want to believe that everything will be all right." He reached for her hand, and she let him have it. It felt good, but she didn't trust her own judgment with men. Last time hadn't turned out so well. After several seconds, she pulled away. He let her with only a small hesitation. "Carol said it took her something like three months to find you."

"I had no idea she was even looking. I hadn't talked to her in a couple of months before all this started. She didn't even know I'd been kicked out of the apartment. Thank God Levi didn't think to park my car out of sight. Carol said that's how she found me. Saw the car in back of the house where she suspected I was, then went investigating. There are windows to the basement at the side of the house where the yard slopes down and is uneven with the rest of the land. After confirming the car was mine, she started looking. I heard her and called out. That's when she broke me out."

"Yeah. We talked to her. She'd taken the Winnebago a few weeks ago, but didn't tell anyone where she was goin'."

"Apparently, she staked out the house for several days. Took her a while because she waited for Levi to leave. That's when she confirmed the car was mine and found me in the basement."

"I take it he didn't leave the house often?"

"No. I was close to delivering. He seemed to be waiting for something. I have no idea what, but the second he had what he wanted, he came at me with the knife. I fought him, and Cheetah heard me screaming. She quit trying to be quiet and broke in the front door. She got to the basement just as he had me pinned down and plunged the knife into me." Helen couldn't help but shiver. She nearly gagged at the memory. The pain had been horrific, not to mention the thought that Levi had hurt her baby. "She attacked him with her bare hands. Fought him like a woman possessed. I've never seen anything like it outside the movies. He still managed to get away, but I think she hurt him. I think Carol would have gone after him if I hadn't been in such bad shape. She got me out of there and drove me here."

"You said you were already several weeks pregnant when all this happened. Where's the father?"

She looked away again, ashamed. "No idea. I met him at a bar. We got drunk and had a good time. Obviously we weren't careful, and the next thing I know, I'm making a few changes to my life." She looked back, needing to judge Trucker's reaction. She didn't expect the big grin she found. "What?"

"Nothin'," he said, raising his hands, a gesture of surrender. "Just thinkin' that if your baby daddy ain't around, that makes my life a lot simpler."

Helen couldn't help it. Her jaw dropped and the breath left her lungs. "How can you even say that? How horrible!" She wanted to punch him right in the mouth. "I'm all alone. My child has no father, and I've just been through the most horrific thing I've ever imagined! How can me not having someone around to protect me and my daughter be a good thing?"

Trucker was completely unapologetic. "Means you'll need someone around to fill that gap." He shrugged. "Sounds like your baby daddy ain't qualified in that department so I'll have to take over."

She blinked, not sure she'd heard him correctly. "I beg your pardon?"

"I said, I'm taking over as your baby daddy." The man was grinning like an ape, obviously finding the whole situation hilarious.

"Would you stop saying 'baby daddy'? I hate that!"

"Sorry. Let me rephrase. I'll be taking over as protector for you and your daughter. You'll stay here with me and the rest of the club, and you'll have all the help and safety you need."

"Do I get a say in this?"

"Do you *want* a say in this?" Again, his gaze was intense. He seemed to look straight into her soul when he wanted to. Helen wanted what he was offering more than just about anything else in the world right now. She wanted that security. But was it real? Had she traded one prison for another? "Or do you want me to make the decision for you?"

"I…"

"That's what I thought. You're afraid, and that's natural. I think you want someone to force your hand." He picked up her hand again, and this time she didn't pull away. "You have to be here for a while anyway to heal. Get to know us. I promise you'll feel better about the whole thing." While he talked to her, he slowly brought her hand to his lips.

When he finished, he kissed her fingers gently, his mouth lingering far longer than she should have let him. Helen's stomach rolled. It was the first intimate contact she'd had since her one-night stand. She tried to put down her reaction to lack of human contact, but she doubted that was the only reason for it.

She *burned* at his simple touch. Shivers raced over her body, and she broke out in a light sweat. Then he turned her hand over and brought her palm to his lips. Inhaling, he closed his eyes and kissed the center. When he exhaled, he opened his eyes and stared straight into hers. There was longing there. Not just a sexual hunger, though that was present too, but something inside him that connected with something inside her. He'd been with her nearly the entire time she'd been at the Bones clubhouse. He'd been unfailingly gentle. He was good with her daughter, whom she'd yet to name. Now, he indicated he wanted to share more with her. Was she ready?

No. Not yet. But she could feel her resistance to him wasn't what it should be. Trucker could break down those walls with little effort. The question was, how long would he try before he gave up? How long did she want to resist him?

Chapter Four

"Are you the owner of that old Winnebago?"

There was a guy in a police uniform outside the clubhouse door. He smiled, looking at ease as he questioned Rain, Arkham's woman. He tried to shoulder his way through the door, but Rain was having none of it. She planted her feet apart and refused to budge an inch. Wiped the smug grin off the bastard's face in a hurry when she didn't let him pass. Since she'd come to stay with them, the girl had shown a profound confidence and a colorful flair that kept them all in stitches.

"Do I look like I'd own that fuckin' piece of shit son of a bitch? It's a Goddamned relic!"

"I... that is, if it's not yours, then who does it belong to?" Between Rain's unmoving stance and belligerent attitude, the officer momentarily lost his sure confidence. Trucker supposed the man was good-looking. Probably had women all over the county swooning wherever he went. Probably got all the information he needed by virtue of his charming personality, megawatt smile, and movie star good looks. If that didn't work, most people would have probably let him in when he advanced on them like he had Rain. She was unaffected by any of it.

"Beats the fuck outta me." Rain slammed the door in his face to the hoots of everyone in the room. Torpedo ruffled her hair as he passed, chuckling. Rain flipped him off. Torpedo opened the door to a scowling officer.

"Why're you interested in the RV?" Torpedo wasn't what one would call a nice man, but he was usually the most diplomatic of the bunch.

"There was a report of a stabbing across town. The perpetrators were seen hauling ass in a vehicle that matches this description."

No one gave any indication, but they were all on alert, paying attention to everything going on. One thing Trucker noticed was the man's lack of a handheld radio. While that didn't necessarily mean anything, a lone officer with no immediate means of calling for help was just a bit unusual. Also, the SUV he was driving was brown with all the appropriate decals and such, but it was a Chevy Tahoe. Pulaski County used Ford Explorers.

"Perpetrators, huh?"

"Yeah. The victim was stabbed multiple times. It's believed his attackers are armed and dangerous."

"How many were there?" Torpedo was fishing. Helen was adamant no police be involved, but hadn't said why. Trucker just assumed it was because she'd been held for so long and no one had shown up to help her, or Redding had threatened her in some way if she'd managed to get to the cops. Did she believe the police were in cahoots with her captor?

"Two. Female. One white. One African-American. We believe it was a robbery gone wrong."

"I see." Torpedo crossed his arms over his chest. "Well, the RV belongs to the club, but the title is in Trucker's name."

"Your boy taken it out recently?" The man smiled congenially, but there was nothing congenial about the look in his eyes. Or the way he held himself. One hand rested on his side arm, and Trucker watched as he used his finger to release the snap strap around his gun for ease of drawing his weapon.

Trucker stood and walked to the door to stand beside Torpedo. Neither man was small. In fact, the officer had to crane his neck to look at either of them. "I'm the *boy* in question," Trucker said, making fists at his sides to make the veins and muscles stand out in his arms, a blatant show of strength. "And no. I've not taken that RV out." Not a lie. Cheetah had, but not him.

The officer continued to smile, but Trucker could see he was rethinking his situation. "We have good information that says your RV was used in a crime. I know Bones MC helps the community from time to time, but I also know you're into some shady shit. If you're making meth in there, I don't much care. I'm not here for a drug bust. I just want to know where the girls who were in that RV a week ago are, and I'm going to have to have a look inside the vehicle to search for them or any evidence they may have left behind."

Trucker heard chairs scraping over the floor as several members stood in support of him and Torpedo. Cain shouldered his way between Trucker and his vice president. "You got a warrant?"

"Look. I'm here as a courtesy to you and your club. If I have to go through the trouble of getting a warrant and bothering a judge, I won't be so nice when I get back."

"Well, that's just too Goddamned bad for you, isn't it?" Cain looked furious. Trucker knew the other man well enough to know it was an act, but the officer didn't. "You want in that RV or any of our property, you get a fuckin' warrant. Otherwise, you can take your sorry ass the Goddamned fuck outta here."

The officer looked ready to do murder, but he backed down. "Once I get the sheriff and a judge involved, I can't help you. You let me in there now, any drug manufacturing is overlooked. Once other officers are involved, all deals are off. If you're hiding those girls, the best thing you can do is hand them over now."

"Go fuck yourself," Cain said before slamming the door. He looked at Torpedo, who nodded. Then he focused on Trucker. "Shit just got real, brother. Your woman needs to tell you everything she can remember. No matter how insignificant. We need to know what we're dealing with sooner rather than later."

"You know that guy ain't a fuckin' cop."

Cain gave him an impatient look. "Cheetah staked out that place for weeks. She made her move when no one would see her because that's the shit we do. You honestly think I don't know she'd be sure to make a clean getaway? 'Cause that woman is one wily cat."

"Our boy, Levi, is the one givin' the description of the RV," Trucker mused. "Barney Fife there knew he was comin' into our territory. Knew who we were but didn't prepare for it."

"Yeah," Torpedo finished. "You'd think he'd'a brought another officer with him."

Trucker growled, his temper spiking. "Exactly what I was thinking. No secret Cheetah's Bones. If Levi and this clown have been around here a while, they'll know that and know she'd come back here."

"Knew this Levi prick couldn't do it all himself. He'd need help for any number of things." Cain crossed the room, headed downstairs to church. "Bring Helen downstairs. We need to get to the bottom of this. She needs to give us all the information she can. Starting with why she doesn't want the police involved."

* * *

"He said he had eyes and ears in the police," Helen whispered. "I was never really sure but was terrified to take a chance."

"So you never actually saw that bastard outside our door, or any other officer?" Cain looked hard as nails. It was difficult to read the man, but she knew he was pissed. She hoped it wasn't at her.

"No. But there was one man who came by several times. He always had a ski mask on so I couldn't see his face. I got the impression he had medical training of some kind. I never let him examine me, and Levi didn't force the issue, saying it wasn't worth harming the baby. The plan was for him to deliver the baby with Levi's help. At least, that's what I think. I only heard bits and pieces of their conversation from the basement. Which is why I was so startled when he came at me. I wasn't expecting anything until they were both in the room."

"I think it's safe to say his help isn't the police." Arkham stood as he spoke, reaching for pictures Data had pulled from the security cameras. "Dumbass ain't driving the right vehicle."

"Facial recognition confirms there isn't anyone on the local sheriff's department resembling this guy," Data said. "I agree with Arkham."

"Facial recognition? You guys can do that?"

Trucker winked at her. "That and more, sweetheart. We're not your normal MC."

"So, that's one problem eliminated." Cain sat back in his chair, crossing his arms over his chest. "Anyone have an objection to us going after this guy? 'Cause this is gonna to be a permanent solution."

Helen looked around her at the stony-faced men. None of them said a word. This was a side of Bones she hadn't seen before. These men were all business. She'd seen them worried, and playing, but this was... this was intense.

"Good. Arkham, take Shadow, Deadeye, and Goose. Be ready to leave in twelve hours. We'll set up surveillance on these motherfuckers. I want both of them at Levi's residence. If they're making a play to get Helen back they're not leaving any time soon, and they'll need to make a plan."

"They have to get her back," Shadow said. "She can identify Levi. If it's his operation, he won't let her go. If the other guy was running the outfit, he'd have just killed Levi, then cut and run."

"OK," Cain said. "Take whatever you need, Arkham. I want a plan to off both those motherfuckers ready to go in twelve hours. We leave in sixteen hours to execute it."

Arkham nodded. The other three men stood, and all four of them left the room. Helen tried not to fidget. Cain had just casually dropped the fact that he intended to kill two men. Had Levi done that, she'd have known he didn't intend to let her live. Trucker moved to her side, wrapping his arm around her shoulders before dropping a kiss on the top of her head.

Cain looked at her. "We'll take care of this, Helen. These fucks ain't gonna get near you again." He glanced at Trucker, nodded once, and then adjourned the group.

Trucker took her hand. "Come on, honey. Let's go to the common room and find something to eat."

"But Mama and Angel are babysitting. I need to relieve them."

He urged her up the stairs. "First of all, there isn't one single woman in this place who wouldn't fight to get to babysit. Second, they're probably in the common room anyway, laughing at the men making baby faces at the little princess. It's what they live for."

* * *

Several hours later, Trucker carried a sleeping Helen -- who carried a sleeping Honey Bunny -- to her room. He took the child from her arms and placed her in the waiting bassinet before kissing the baby's forehead and stroking the downy-soft shock of dark hair. OK, so Helen hadn't actually named the child Honey Bunny. That was just what she called her for now. For some reason, Helen was reluctant to actually name the child. Mama had volunteered to do the necessary paperwork to get the birth certificate, but Helen still hadn't given the child a real name.

"Trucker?" Helen's voice was sleepy. Sexy. God, he was in trouble! She'd reached out to him. Had called his name to assure herself things were good.

"Hi, baby," he said, sitting on the side of the bed. He stroked her hair, smoothing it back from her face. "Go back to sleep. The little princess is fine. Warm and content."

She reached up and circled his wrist with her small hand. "Will you stay with us tonight?" This startled Trucker. It must have shown on his face because she hastily released him and added. "You don't have to. I - I just --"

He cut her off with a quick kiss. A firm but gentle pressing of his lips to hers. It was meant only to silence her, but the damage was done. It took everything in Trucker for him not to deepen his kiss. His lips tingled where they touched hers. She trembled beneath him but didn't pull away, her hand tightening on his wrist. Trucker gritted his teeth and kept it light, but he had no idea how he managed.

Ending that kiss was one of the hardest things Trucker had ever done. He wanted this woman with everything in him, but not now. She was still healing from physical and psychological wounds he couldn't fathom. Now, she needed tender care. Mama was right. He needed to be her rock. Not a boulder smashing into her life.

"Never be afraid to ask me for anything, Helen," he said, placing his forehead against hers. "You need somethin', I'm here for you."

Wide-eyed, she placed trembling fingers to her lips. "You kissed me," she whispered.

He grinned. "I did. I won't do it again if you don't want me to, but I wanted the privilege of doing it once. Didn't want to risk you saying no."

"I… OK," Helen said. "Only…"

When she didn't continue, Trucker gently asked, "Only what, baby?"

"Well, will you do it again?"

With a smile, he said, "It would be my sincerest pleasure."

Her arms came around his neck as she tilted her face up to him. Lips parting, she welcomed him eagerly. Trucker grunted as she opened for him, sweeping his tongue inside to dance with hers wickedly. Whimpers escaped from Helen as he continued with languid strokes of his tongue against hers. When she subtly rocked her hips beside him, Trucker slid one hand down her hip to her thigh and back. She was clothed in yoga pants and a T-shirt, comfortable clothing for ease of movement and that didn't aggravate her surgical site. It was that reminder alone that made Trucker keep his aggression in check. Everything male inside him was screaming at him to claim his woman. But he couldn't. Not now. Soon, but not now.

He ended the kiss with a groan of despair. God, he wanted her! "Jesus," he whispered. "What the fuck am I gonna do with you, baby?"

"Why'd you stop? You know I want you, too." She sounded faintly hurt, out of breath and needy in her lust.

"Not because I wanted to stop," he answered. Unable to resist, he trailed kisses down her neck to her shoulder. She shivered, and her fingers tightened in the hair at the nape of his neck. "Mama would have my hide if she found out I fucked you before she gave the OK."

Helen blushed. He felt her skin heat as he continued to lick and nip at her neck, scraping his short beard over her delicate flesh. "You talk to her about your sex life?"

He chuckled. "Only because you've been through some pretty significant trauma, baby. If I didn't wait to get her clearance, she'd beat me to a bloody pulp, and she should. I'm not taking any chances on hurting you."

"What if I wanted you anyway?"

"God, Helen. Don't fuckin' tempt me. It's hard enough as it is. You're too important to me to risk it."

"But --"

"I'll talk to Mama tomorrow. If you think I'll wait one second more than I have to, you're fuckin' crazy."

She giggled, not loosening her hold on him. "You're the crazy one."

Trucker worked his lips around her neck to kiss her chin, then her nose. "I've never felt saner in my life, Helen."

"Am I really important to you? I mean, you've *made* yourself important to me. I've never had a man treat me so good in my whole life. All I've done for you is bring trouble to your door."

Trucker thought about it awhile. Why did he feel so strongly for her? Was it that she was a damsel in distress? No. He flatly rejected that notion because he'd always believed his woman needed to be strong. He wanted her to rely on him, but with ExFil and the runs he did for Bones, any woman in his life had to understand his life wasn't pretty. He had no idea what kind of life Helen had before all this happened to her, but he thought it was pretty normal.

"There's something inside you, Helen. You're vulnerable, but resolved. You're a survivor. You showed that by making it this far and not allowing anyone to kill you or your child."

"I'm not sure I really had anything to do with that. If Carol hadn't come along, there wouldn't have been much I could have done about it."

"Maybe not, but you fought. Cheetah told us you were fightin' with all you had in you, considerin' you were so far into your pregnancy."

She sighed. "Are you guys really going to kill Levi and his friend?"

"We are. Since the hit is inside our territory, Cain excluded me from the operation, so I'll be stayin' here with you. Torpedo is leadin' the group. They're all restin' up right now. Should be leavin' to take care of that motherfucker in about eight hours or so."

"I don't want anyone hurt on my account. I want Levi dead more than just about anything, and I'm not sure how I feel about that, but I know I could never live with myself if someone from Bones was hurt because of this."

"Don't worry your pretty head about that, baby. Sometimes things go wrong. No matter how much you prepare for a mission, the situation is always fluid. You have to adapt. This group is the best there is at adapting. Ain't sayin' it won't happen, but I can tell you that, if it does, no one here will begrudge it."

"How can you say that? I don't want anyone harmed because of me!"

"Honey, we're not just an MC. Every one of us belongs to Cain's paramilitary outfit, ExFil. Every one of us has risked our lives for trivial things people believe to be important. Protecting one of our own, a mother and her child, is more important than anything we've ever been hired to take on. You're worth it."

Without another word, Helen sat up and reached for him. She slid her arms around him and hugged him fiercely. Her slight body trembled as she clung to him. "Thank you so much, Trucker. I need to thank everyone here. You've all been so good to me. I've never felt more accepted and more like I matter than I have while here. Mama, Carol, Pops, everyone. Most especially you. You've been with me every single second you could, and I want you to know I appreciate it."

"You're very welcome, baby." He kissed her again, this time lingering softly, but not stoking the fire he knew was smoldering inside them both.

"So, you'll stay with me tonight?"

Trucker laughed. "Honey, wild horses couldn't drag me away. Scoot over."

She did, and Trucker slid in beside her. As if it were the most natural thing in the world, Helen cuddled into his side, resting her head on his chest. Trucker wrapped both his arms around her and kissed the top of her head. It wasn't long before she drifted off.

Helen's breaths, deep and even, feathered over Trucker's chest. Nothing had ever felt so right. His woman. In his arms. Next to them in the little bassinette lay her child. His child. In his heart he'd already laid a claim to that little girl, and he'd always think of her as his.

A couple of hours passed before he heard the little princess start stirring. The child was nothing if not punctual. Every three hours, on the dot, she woke, dictating it was time to eat. Helen hadn't moved after she'd dozed off, indicating she had to be exhausted.

Before the baby could create her usual ruckus, Trucker slipped from the bed, covering Helen and kissing her temple. He picked up the child as she squirmed, trying to wake herself to eat. He snagged a couple of diapers and a blanket before leaving to go to the kitchen. Helen kept chilled and frozen milk ready for use when she couldn't breastfeed.

Trucker held the child in one arm while preparing a bottle in the other, setting it down in warm water to heat it while he changed the baby. All the while, he talked to her. Yeah, it was baby talk, but it kept the child from fussing too much until he could get her bottle ready.

Once she was changed and the bottle heated to the perfect temperature, Trucker took the child back to Helen's room. He sat in the chair and fed her, talking softly to her the whole time. Once she finished, he put her on his shoulder and patted her back gently until she gave a very unladylike and very impressive burp. He praised her, rubbing her back with gentle circles of his big palm.

"That's my girl. That one came from waaaay down, didn't it? Feel better now?" The child cooed before settling to sleep. Trucker chuckled.

"Is she hungry?" Helen propped herself up on an elbow, obviously not completely awake yet.

"She's fine, honey. I got her took care of."

"You did?"

"Hey. I'm a whiz at taking care of my girls." He laid the baby in her bed gently before going back to her mother. "You need rest if you're going to heal, so I admit my motives may have been a little selfish."

Helen giggled. "You're so bad."

"Maybe, but I think you like me bad. Besides, I think the princess over there likes me, too."

"She's too little to know what she likes." Helen reached for him as he climbed into bed beside her. Once settled, she looked up at him with a beautiful, soft smile. "Thank you, Trucker. For everything."

"Nothin' to thank me for." He settled beside Helen, pulling her close. "I'm glad I could help. Thanks for letting me help with the little one." He kissed her forehead. "Which, by the way, you decided on a name for her yet?"

Helen didn't look at him, only shrugged. "Not yet. I'll come up with something soon."

Trucker was silent for a moment, the real reason she hadn't named her daughter hitting him like a hammer to an anvil. "You're afraid to name her until Levi's threat is gone. Aren't you?" He spoke quietly, gently. The last thing he wanted to do was bungle this after that first day in Mama's clinic.

To his complete and utter horror, Helen dissolved into tears.

Chapter Five

"I want in, Cain."

Cain didn't look up from where he was going over their plan of attack one last time. "You know I can't allow that. Too close to home for it to be personal. He comes back to the clubhouse, have at him. Otherwise, you're off this."

"I can't stay here and do nothing. She needs me to be there with you."

"She needs you to be the last line of defense between her and Bunny Girl."

"Cain, she's afraid to name the child because Levi's still out there. I can't stand seeing her cry over this!"

"It will all be over soon. If it helps, be there with Data when it goes down. He'll have eyes and ears on us at all times."

"If it were Angel, would you sit it out willingly?"

Cain finally stopped what he was doing and gave his brother a hard look. "I'm president of this club, Trucker. I get you. I do. But we've had too many close calls here lately. It's bad enough I'm getting the club involved when one of those fuckers we're getting ready to off was on our property. Redding's henchman might not be in the sheriff's department, but if the bastards are missed, the real police will come knocking if they backtrack 'em. I'm doin' it because it's the right thing to do. That woman and her child will never be safe until this is done. Now, I'm askin' you to respect me in this. Be with your woman. Take her mind off this, 'cause I know it's all she's thinkin' about right now. Play with her child. Solidify your place in her life, because there is no question in my mind you're the man for her."

Trucker laced his fingers behind his neck, head down as he tried to stem his frustration. "When do you guys leave?"

Cain didn't answer for a long moment. "Not sure. We're still planning. I'm going through several different scenarios to see which poses the least risk with the maximum chance of success. I don't want anything leading back to us."

Trucker took a deep breath. "Fine. I'm sorry. You understand where I'm coming from?"

"I do. If I were in your shoes, I'd sure as hell want fuckin' payback. But I have to protect everyone involved. That includes your woman. And you." He punched Trucker's shoulder firmly. "You get me?"

"I do."

"Then please, Trucker. Stay here with your woman."

Cain never said "please" in regard to an order. You followed his orders or you were out. The fact that he did this time told Trucker the man truly understood how he felt. It was that knowledge more than anything that gave him the strength to sit this one out.

After taking several deep breaths and walking around the clubhouse a few times to find some kind of calm, Trucker went back inside. He found Helen with her daughter in the common room. Suzie, one of the teenagers who'd "adopted" the club back in the summer, was holding the baby while Helen showed her how to give the girl a bottle. Stunner sat in a nearby chair, his body firmly between Suzie and any entrance to the room. For once, he didn't sport glitter or any other kind of coloring to his hair and beard. After the incident at Christmas, Suzie had stopped decorating the big man. Whether it was her own choosing or because of what Pig had said to her before

Stunner had beaten him to a bloody pulp, Trucker didn't know. The only thing he knew for sure was the incident in question had changed Suzie. She threw herself into schoolwork and pestered Data constantly for lessons on the computer, not that the other man minded. Through it all, Stunner remained at her side, guarding her.

Trucker couldn't help but grin. Helen looked right at home with her arm around Suzie as she encouraged the teenager. He met Stunner's eye, and the other man gave a curt nod as if to say, "All's well."

After that, Trucker wasn't sure exactly what to do. Normally, he'd be planning with his brothers, but club policy with shit like this was the less anyone not involved knows, the better. He'd sure as shit listen in when they hit the place, but he wouldn't be part of actually setting things up. Battle planning wasn't his best asset. He was the weapons man. The one who could fix anything. He knew what the team would need and had already prepared the chase vehicle. He'd checked and rechecked everything, making the team as ready as they could be.

Deciding he needed some physical activity, he went out the back to the gym. They'd set up equipment in a barn next to the clubhouse. It was cold this time of year, but had everything he needed for a vigorous workout.

Deciding the heavy bag would be perfect for this situation, he wrapped his hands and began pounding away his frustration. Not being part of this felt like letting Helen down. Made him feel like less of a man. He had no problem letting his brothers help, but he hated being out of the ride completely. Sure, he could sit with Data in his command center with all the readouts from body cams and the audio, but he knew

Cain didn't really want him there. He wanted him out of it in case things went to shit. Even though his relationship with Helen was still new and unknown by anyone outside the club, he couldn't imagine Helen being cooped up in the clubhouse for the rest of her life. And there was a matter of the baby. At some point, there would have to be a birth certificate. Even with Mama fudging the actual date of birth, the child would still be a trail leading back to Levi, should something happen that Bones was unable to make him disappear completely.

So here he was. Beating the fuck out of the heavy bag until sweat poured down his body and his hands ached despite the padding.

"Trucker?"

Fuck. Helen's soft voice penetrated his concentration. No matter what he was doing or how much he was concentrating on anything, that woman could pierce through to capture his attention. Normally, he'd welcome her presence. She soothed him as much as she inflamed him. Not tonight. Not when his club was riding into danger on his woman's behalf and wouldn't let him join.

"Not now, Helen." He continued to pound the bag mercilessly, grunting with each hit or kick.

She was silent for a long while. So long Trucker thought she'd gone. He knew better, but he'd hoped. Helen needed to heal, not be here with him in this state. If she were whole, he'd lose himself in her body, if she'd have him. He thought she might, but now wasn't the time.

"Did I do something wrong?"

Fuck. She sounded forlorn. Hurt. Trucker stopped and hugged the bag, leaning his weight into it slightly. "No, baby. It's not you." His lungs were heavy with his exertion. It felt good, but not as fulfilling as he'd hoped.

"Oh. I -- I misunderstood last night. I thought we were going to try... I don't know, *something* together."

"No. You didn't misunderstand."

"What is it then?"

He went back to punching the bag, albeit with less vigor. No reason to terrify the woman. "Nothing. I just need --" *punch, punch*, "some time alone." *Punch, kick, punch, punch.*

Again, he thought she'd left, but then he felt her soft palm on his bare skin, curling around his shoulder. Trucker's first instinct was to shrug her off, but he couldn't. He craved her touch any way he could get it. Gradually, he stopped, still breathing hard. Turning to face her wasn't even an option. She'd see right through him, see the need he knew was shining in his eyes. Not only would it be an inappropriate time for her, it would be purely selfish on his part. Though he wanted to resist her, when she urged him to face her, he couldn't.

There was a quiet understanding in Helen's sea-green eyes, as if she understood perfectly the war raging inside him. Instead of backing off when Trucker let his intense need of her show when he held her gaze, Helen slid her hand from his shoulder to his heaving, sweating chest.

"Let's take a shower," she said softly. "Will you come with me?"

He wanted to deny her, actually looked back at the bag, halfheartedly raising an arm to punch at the bag once. Then he allowed her to lead him back inside and upstairs to her room.

* * *

Helen might still be healing from the trauma she'd endured a week ago, but she was no shrinking violet. One thing she'd come to realize over her time with Trucker was that she wanted to see where this thing with him led. He'd accepted her and her baby already. She just had no idea how far he was willing to go. She suspected he wasn't going anywhere. Not many men she knew would willingly change a dirty diaper if there were any other option. Trucker didn't even flinch.

She led him to the shower in her room where he quickly took over, adjusting the water to the desired temperature. Though she knew he needed this, Helen was still hesitant about undressing. Not only was she adjusting to her body's changes after birth, but she was going to have a wicked scar. It would probably fade in time, but right now it was still healing.

Trucker didn't seem concerned, though. He shucked his clothing quickly then helped with hers. All the while, he didn't say a word.

His body was muscled and battle-scarred from cuts and what she suspected was a couple of bullet wounds. Tattoos surrounded or covered some of the scars, but not as much as she'd have thought. The man was definitely an impressive male specimen.

Stepping into the shower, Helen took Trucker's hand and pulled him in after her. His hands automatically went to her waist as he looked down into her face. His jaw clenched reflexively, the muscle there bulging as his teeth ground together.

"Sit," she said, motioning to the bench running the length of the back of the shower. It was large enough for a showerhead at either end. While Trucker had set one, Helen now adjusted the other. The spray didn't quite reach the middle of the bench where he sat, but mist dampened him.

Helen was acutely aware of him watching her every move. When she turned to face him fully, she held his gaze boldly.

"I'm sorry," she said as she approached him. "It's obvious you're hurting, and I don't know why. But I want to help." When he opened his mouth, she stopped him. "No. You don't have to explain. Just know that I'm here when you're ready. For now, though, let's just enjoy the moment."

That seemed to be the exact right thing to say because he relaxed. She could tell he wasn't completely satisfied yet, but maybe, after she'd distracted him for a while, he'd decide to confide in her.

Helen picked up a bottle of shower gel, squirted a generous amount into her hand, and lathered it between her palms. She watched as Trucker's body gradually dampened in the mist of the spray. Then she leaned over. Her breasts were inches from him, but he didn't move to touch her. His eyes were glued to her chest though. She couldn't help but grin.

Kneeling in front of Trucker, Helen glided her slick palms over his damp chest in gentle strokes. His arms were next. As far as she could reach on her knees between his legs. That big cock of his was long and thick, standing proudly at attention, but still he didn't move to touch her. She wasn't deterred. He clearly wanted her touch. Wanted her.

"I'll apologize in advance if things get a little messy. The hot water sometimes makes my breasts drip." She grinned up at him, hoping for a smile. Instead, there was a flash of heat there.

"That supposed to make me behave?"

She shook her head. "No one said I wanted you to behave. Just not to be offended if things get a little messy."

Mist sprayed over them enough to gently rinse the soap from Trucker's body. Helen didn't rush things. In fact, she wanted to prolong the situation if she could.

"Messy sex is always the best sex." His voice was deep and gruff, husky with his arousal. Helen got a little thrill that she was able to affect him as much as he affected her. His hands gripped the bench until his knuckles turned white, the muscles in his arms standing out in stark relief.

She slid down his body, finding his gaze with hers and locking on. While she didn't feel particularly sexy, Trucker looked at her as if he were starving for her, as if it was everything he could do not to touch her. His jaw bunched at the side of his face where he clenched his teeth repeatedly. Helen imagined he was hanging on to his control by sheer force of will. Perhaps he was. But she knew enough to know this man wanted her in a primal way. Whatever the reason, he'd made up his mind to have her. She was about to test his control even knowing she was limited in what she could do with him at the moment. Why? Because she'd decided he was hers. She wanted Trucker for her own, and she'd do whatever she could to win him.

* * *

Trucker knew he should push Helen away. This was the worst idea ever, but his fucking hands wouldn't be pried from the bench to end this. He watched in rapt fascination as she sank lower and lower until he felt her warm breath feather over the head of his cock. Her eyes were glued to his, not blinking or wavering in the least. She was watching him as intently as he was watching her, only she was the one with all the power while he had none. He was hers to do with as she pleased.

Which led to a most pressing question. One that could make or break him. It was the only thing short of an all-out battle that allowed him to stop her.

"Helen, baby. Stop a second."

She blinked up at him. Though she didn't lower her mouth to him -- to both his complete frustration and utter relief -- she grasped his cock in her soft palm to make slow, lazy pumps up his rigid length. She looked expectant but wary, as if she weren't sure she wanted to obey him but needed to know what he had to say. "What is it?"

"Baby, as much as I want this -- and I *really* want this -- I have to know why. I don't want you doing something you're uncomfortable with."

"Why do you think I'm doing it?" She gave him an enigmatic little smile.

"I don't know," he growled. "That's why I'm fuckin' askin'!" He was surprised when she giggled, her smile now lighting up her face.

"I'm doing it because you need it. You want to be out there with your brothers so you have their backs. I'm not sure why Cain won't let you, but I suspect it's because of me. And, yes, I know you'd be out there unless it was Cain who called you off so don't try to pretend you weren't ordered to stay behind." She rubbed one hand up and down his thigh now, the other still lazily stroking his cock. "I can't have sex with you yet. I haven't healed enough from the birth. But I can give you this." She leaned down and swiped the head of his cock with her tongue. "In fact, I insist on it."

"Wait." His command sounded strangled and not nearly as forceful as he'd intended it to. "Don't do this because you think you owe me, Helen. I'll be here no matter what. I can't seem to help myself. You and the baby are very important to me. I want…" He swallowed, wincing at how whipped he sounded. The guys were right. He was completely pussy-whipped. Without getting the pussy. "I want you to be part of my life. No matter what happens after this."

"No worries there, big guy." She smiled up at him, her little pink tongue making another swipe. "You treat us right, and we'll stick around a long time. Then you can look forward to fighting off boys who try to date your girl."

He groaned in defeat. "You're fighting on two fronts, Helen. No fair."

"I'm simply stating the facts as I see them. You want me. I want you. I can see by your actions you want more than sex. I'm willing to give it a try if you are. And I've never seen a man willingly change a dirty diaper who wasn't all in. You may not acknowledge it, but that more than anything convinces me you really want something more."

"Fuck," he said, relaxing his grip on the bench. "You win."

Trucker reached for her, threading his fingers through her hair before pulling her up to him for a searing kiss. She tasted like heaven. Paradise. She was everything he'd ever wanted in a woman. Helen was strong but vulnerable in a way. She needed his protection but was perfectly capable of taking care of herself. The situation she'd found herself in was impossible, but she'd managed to land on her feet with only a little help. Now, she was the one taking control and Trucker was good with that.

She kissed him back with a passion to match his own, never once pushing away or denying him. Trucker knew she was intent on oral sex, but he was hesitant. Not because he didn't want it. Because he wasn't sure what would be comfortable for her, and he couldn't stand the idea of not pleasuring her back.

When he finally let the kiss end, she grinned up at him before sinking back to her knees. Never taking her gaze from his, Helen engulfed his cock in the wet cavern of her mouth. She took him down as far as she could go. He felt the back of her throat as her tongue slid along his length. Trucker couldn't help the thrust of his hips or the gasps from his throat. Her mouth on him was sinful. Wicked.

That was it. He couldn't take anymore. Pulling her up with a gentle tug on her hair, he pulled her onto his lap, then turned them so she was lying on the bench with him on top of her.

"I know I can't fuck you," he growled, "but you're gonna come with me."

"Trucker." Her soft gasp was sweet music. She had a confused look on her face that morphed into surprised delight when he aligned his cock with her clit and slid over her, rubbing the little bud over and over.

"I'm not comin' till you do, baby," he said. "Now, move with me."

She did. It didn't take her long to find the position and perfect amount of friction for both of them. He knew she had it when her eyes widened and she whimpered. Her gasps and little cries echoed in the shower around them, the water hitting the tiles and their wet skin the perfect harmony to her melody. Trucker couldn't think past the dazed, wide-eyed look on her lovely face.

Helen wrapped her legs around him, locking her ankles at the small of his back. Her heels dug in as if to spur him on until her breathing was ragged and she bucked hard against him.

Trucker was about to lose his mind with the need to come. It took every ounce of willpower and discipline he had not to simply angle his cock down just that little bit and sink into her heat. Had he not been afraid he'd hurt her, he might have. He knew she was still tender from everything and had no idea how much pain she was in even now. The only thing that comforted him was how tightly she clung to him and how sinuously she moved under him. She was as lost as he was.

Just when he was afraid he couldn't take another second, Helen tensed. Her muscles tightened then she arched her back and screamed. That was his OK to let himself go. His hoarse bellow followed her scream, and he came over her belly with spurt after spurt of hot seed.

Heart pounding, breath coming in ragged gasps, Trucker pulled Helen into his arms so that she straddled him. He wrapped his arms tightly around her while they recovered. Helen's arms were twined around his neck, clinging to him sweetly. Her breath feathered over the pulse at his neck.

After a while, he kissed her hair. "You good, baby?"

"I am. Thank you."

"I'm the one who should be thanking *you*. Wasn't expecting this kind of action today." He tried to make light of the situation, but now that the post-orgasmic bliss was fading, Trucker was beginning to feel the weight of his responsibilities again. Rather, the lack of responsibilities. He really wanted to be out there with his brothers.

"Give it another couple of weeks or so. There'll be more days like this. That is, if you want it." She looked up at him, leaning in to kiss his chin.

"Always, baby. This and much, much more."

Chapter Six

Cain returned late the next day with the rest of the crew, all of them grim-faced. "What happened?" Trucker demanded. Cain gave him a quelling look but jerked his head toward the basement door. Time for church.

Every patched member who was in the common room, plus Cheetah, stopped what they were doing and filed downstairs. Except for Stunner. He remained with Suzie where the girl cast a nervous look up at him. The big man grunted, but remained seated. Trucker glanced around. Unless something changed, the women were all with Helen in the baby's room decorating and putting up the baby bed for when the child was moved into the separate bedroom in Helen's suite. She'd want to know what was going on, but Trucker wanted to know first so he could decide how to tell her. He needed the raw version. He'd give Helen only as much as he thought she could handle. She had enough stress in her life right now without hearing bad news about her abductor.

"Good news and bad news," Cain said when they were all downstairs and the door locked for church. "Good news is Levi's buddy's dead. Levi shot him in the head from the back. He put him in a freezer in the cellar of the new digs he commandeered. I don't imagine he'll get rid of him for a while. Probably waiting to see if he's missed. Kinda like he did when Cheetah sprung Helen. He's either methodical or indecisive. I can't decide which."

"I take it the bad news is Levi's still alive?" Trucker leaned his elbows on the table.

"Yes. We've got Shadow, Arkham, and Sword staking the place out. It's pretty remote. Only way he has electricity is the generator he stole. He's starting to get sloppy. Making mistakes he's not made before." Cain nodded at Data. "You got any insight here?"

"Well, he's never been to a place as off the beaten path as Somerset. Sure, it's pretty close to the interstate and is a good-sized town, but everything around it is rural Kentucky. I think he's bitten off more than he can chew. He's stuck. He doesn't know the places to dispose of a body, and he doesn't know the local underground. I think he came here out of desperation."

"Explain."

"I found some incidents leading up to Helen's that didn't work out the same. The two most recent resulted in the death of both mothers and babies. One before that where the mother survived initially but the child didn't." Several of the guys shifted uncomfortably. No one liked this. "In all three cases, it looked like he was interrupted and had to leave before the procedure was complete. He shot the woman who survived before bugging out. The babies died because he botched the procedure in his haste. This was all highly publicized. I'm surprised we haven't heard more, even though it didn't happen in this state."

"You got ideas about any of it?"

Data held Cain's gaze. "The three incidents were in Florida, and Southern and Northern Georgia respectively. I think someone was on to him. More? I think they were driving him straight to us."

"Jesus," Cain swore softly. He glanced at Storm. "Brother, if this is your father-in-law again, I will beat that motherfucker into oblivion."

"If it is, El Diablo hasn't said anything. Magenta has spoken to him a couple of times. She'd've told me."

"He's trying to force us into a corner for some reason. He wants something from us, and I won't rest easy until I know what." Cain stood, pacing the length of the room and back. "We've got eyes on that little fuck, Redding, for now. We'll keep watch. As long as he stays put in the woods, we can contain this. Until we know who's after him, we maintain distance. The last thing I want is for us to walk into some kind of set-up."

"And if he makes a run for it?" Torpedo asked the question quietly, probably already knowing the answer, just needing to hear it officially.

"I don't want him out there harming others." Cain breathed out a harsh gust of air, his features hard. "Shadow him. But if there is any danger whatsoever of him giving us the slip, waste the motherfucker. Shooter's discretion."

"I don't like this," Trucker muttered. This wasn't his area. He was support. Torpedo and Bohannon did tactics. Cain measured the tactical gain with the collateral loss. The needs of the club came first, but in this case Trucker was worried more about Helen and her child than Bones. "If he's found dead here and Helen's story comes out -- and let's face it, when the baby shows up in the system someone is going to put two and two together -- she's going to be right in the middle of a murder investigation."

"No worries on that account. Mama is perfectly qualified and credentialed for a home delivery. Helen will never be linked with his death."

"Also, if El Diablo did drive that fucker this way, he put him on a path straight to Helen." That more than anything was enough to infuriate Trucker.

"I know, brother. It's the first thing I intend to bring up in our little conversation."

"Fucker needs to disappear," Trucker insisted. "Fast."

Sword snorted. "Which one?"

Cain crossed to him. Trucker could see the understanding on his face as well as the firm resolve. "We'll get Levi, Trucker. But first, I need to have a discussion with El Diablo. If he's maneuvered us into this, I need to know why and what he's gaining. I won't be a pawn for another club or anyone else."

Trucker nodded. "Understood."

"Good. Everything is in place then. We'll keep watch on him in teams of three. Twelve-hour shifts. I want everyone on alert until then. We may need a quick cleanup. If so, we'll need to scour that fuckin' house clean. Questions?" When no one said anything, Cain dismissed them. "Get some rest, people. It's gonna be a long few days. Data, I wanna talk to El Diablo. Now."

Data gave Trucker a knowing look, understanding his brother would want to be in on this. "Give me a few minutes," Data said. "You can take the call in my office."

Trucker followed Data, not giving Cain the opportunity to deny him. Better to ask forgiveness than permission. "If that son of a bitch put a psycho in our territory, I'll kill the motherfucker myself," Trucker muttered as they entered Data's office.

"You'll do what I tell you to," Cain snapped. "And right now, you're here because I understand how you feel about Helen. You want some answers, and I'm willing to let you get them firsthand and even ask questions of your own. But you answer to me, Trucker. *Me.*"

They stared at each other for long moments, neither man backing down. There was a rage burning inside Trucker he'd never known was there when he thought that everything that had happened to Helen might have been caused by the meddling of that bastard El Diablo. He'd been friends with Cain for more years than he cared to think about. They'd served together. They worked together. Now they were members of Bones. Together. In all that time, Trucker had always willingly followed Cain, no matter where he led. This would be no exception. No matter how much he wanted to fuck someone up.

"You're right," Trucker said. "I'm sorry, Cain."

"Good. I'm gonna need everyone on board with this. We're a team."

"Noted. I'm with you, brother."

"I got El Diablo, Cain," Data said.

"Speaker."

A moment later El Diablo's voice filled the room. Instead of his usual witty banter and vaguely condescending attitude, the man sounded completely serious.

"Cain. I'd apologize for the trouble I brought down on your club, but I had nowhere else to drive the man."

"You know, there are numerous swamps in Florida where the gators would have taken care of that particular problem."

"I've only been here a couple months. I'm still learning the finer points of where and how to hide a body in this place."

"You know, you allowed that man to prey on any number of women on his journey here. You willingly put every pregnant woman in his path in danger." Cain looked as angry as he sounded. "Hell, you could have gotten the local heat involved!"

"It's all political, Cain. You know that. I couldn't get rid of him here, but I knew you could."

"Anything you *think* I owe you wasn't worth this, you bastard. We nearly lost a woman and her child here. You sent a murderer straight to our doorstep!"

"I know, I know. You're a hundred percent right."

"What if it had been your own daughter --"

"Stop there, Cain." El Diablo was forceful. "I'm fully aware of the ramifications of my actions. I gave you and your club my complete trust. I put my faith in your skills. That you were really as good as you said you were."

"You could have reached out to us. You know, given us a bit of a heads-up."

"I tried! My protégée said Data wouldn't take his calls!" The man sounded more than a little frustrated and distressed.

"You had a straight line to Magenta, man. You could have gone through her."

"Never!" El Diablo bit out the word with more vehemence than Trucker had heard the man use since they'd met months ago. "I never want this kind of thing to touch her! If that means I put innocents between danger and her, then I'm willing to risk it."

"That's the difference between us and you," Cain said. "We're not what anyone would call fine, law-abiding, upstanding citizens. But we're not monsters. Ever think there's a reason Magenta has kept her distance? Deep down, she knows you're no good for her."

"Leave my daughter out of this, Cain! I will not apologize for protecting her."

"You mean protecting yourself. You don't want her to see the real you because you know she'll cut you out completely."

There was a long pause. So long Trucker thought El Diablo might have hung up on them. "If you have nothing important to discuss, Cain, I'm going." Now, the man sounded ice cold. "Perhaps, from now on, we should establish a direct line between our clubs. You know. In order to avoid situations such as this."

"We have no reason for it. You're the one who keeps coming to us."

"I am," he said without hesitation. "Perhaps that's because I refuse to believe my daughter doesn't want to give me a chance to be in her life. Maybe I just see something in you and your club I recognize in myself. Whatever my motives, rest assured you'd be better off having me as an uneasy ally than an outright enemy."

"That sounds like a threat." Cain leaned over, bracing his hands on the table as he hovered over the speakerphone.

"Take it as you will." El Diablo ended the call.

"Well, that could have gone better," Torpedo groused. He scrubbed his hands over his face. "So, El Diablo and Black Reign purposely drove that fucker this way." He and Cain held gazes for a long time. "Cain, I know you don't like it, but I don't think the man truly mean any ill will. I think he was at a loss. If, as he alluded to before, there's a possibility he's being hunted by his own enemies, he'd want to be sure not to make a known kill before he's established and has his territory protected. He may have loved ones he's more worried about than bystanders."

Cain gave him an annoyed look. "Whose side you on, anyway, pal?"

"You know I'm on yours." Torpedo, ever the diplomat, was trying to smooth things over. They all knew El Diablo posed a significant threat, even from

Florida, but now wasn't the time to discuss it. "I'm just saying don't judge him until we've had a chance to go over all the facts and evaluate them."

Cain looked to Data. "Zora really try to contact you?"

Data shrugged. "Once I found out she was in league with El Diablo, I cut ties. I still monitor her, but I don't share or talk with her."

"Maybe you should rethink that situation. Keep your friends close..."

"Your enemies in your back pocket. Right."

"Something like that." Cain took a breath, looking at each man. "We've got Redding covered tight right now. Yes?"

"Shadow, Arkham, and Bohannon currently." Torpedo's answer was immediate. "Sword, Viper, and me will be relieving them in another eight hours."

"Hold on." That was Pops. Trucker turned to find the older man descending the stairs. Though Trucker knew him to be in his sixties, the man didn't look it. He was fit, if completely gray-headed. Muscle roped his arms and chest, filling out the T-shirt he wore. Gray hair or not, he looked like a warrior. "You boys're overthinking this." His voice was rough, almost like a loud growl.

Cain cocked his head. "Really? How's that?"

"Data. What's the weather bringin'?" Pops locked gazes with Cain.

"There's supposed to be storms moving in soon." Data looked startled as he consulted his phone. "I'll do some looking, but local forecasts are currently giving a shit-ton of snow coming down from the north. Near blizzard-like conditions, followed by intense cold. Subzero temps over several days after this storm. Arctic blast, they're calling it. Cold's supposed to last at least a week before letting up. Even then, it all depends on the strength of the next front. Or some shit." He looked up at Cain. "Ain't no fuckin' meteorologist, bro."

Pause.

"Maybe we won't have to kill him outright." Cain and Pops never looked away from each other as Cain spoke. After about half a minute, Cain's face transformed into an evil grin.

Chapter Seven

The storm was on track to make its way through Somerset and the greater Lake Cumberland area in five days. In a way it was maddening to have to wait that long, but Bones also had only five days to gain the trust of Levi enough that he willingly came to the Boneyard. The Boneyard was the bar owned by the club and used as a neutral place to do business for bikers all over the state.

Fortunately, Bones had a prospect itching to make up for what he thought of as a failure on his part. Clutch had been tasked with making sure Bohannon's woman, Luna, stayed put in the room Bohannon had put her in. She hadn't gotten past Clutch, but had exited through a window where two other prospects, Kickstand and Pig, had been the ones to let her escape go unnoticed. Kickstand had straightened up since then. He was still a fuck-up from time to time, but it wasn't because he wasn't trying make up for his mistakes. He was just young. Pig, on the other hand, had been falling back into his old pattern of dumbassedness when he picked on the wrong girl. He'd made the colossal mistake of ridiculing Suzie and really giving her a hard time. Stunner, one of their youngest patched members at twenty-five, took exception to his treatment of the eleven-year-old. Stunner had beaten Pig mercilessly, giving the young man a concussion and several facial fractures. He was healing nicely, but had straightened up comparatively. At least, for a while. As with all fuckturds, once the immediate threat had passed, they got cocky again. Trucker knew it was only a matter of time before Pig either got another beating or was banned from the club altogether. The only thing saving him currently was that he was related to Arkham. Arkham protected his family, and Bones had followed suit. But Cain would only allow so much. Pig's time was about up.

Clutch was in his late twenties and had been hired at ExFil two years earlier. He'd been invited as a prospect for Bones about six months afterwards. Apparently the young man suffered from PTSD and had refused help. Cain, like always, took over and forced the issue. Not by making him join a therapy group or anything, but by bringing him to Bones. Not a single patched member didn't understand what Clutch was going through. He'd really flourished since he'd joined Bones. As a result, he'd taken that incident as a personal failure. Instead of wallowing in self-pity, though, he'd been eager to atone, volunteering for extra duty and training hard every day. Once the guy learned how to ride a bike without riding the clutch so hard, he'd be golden.

Now, he was the one volunteering to establish a rapport with Levi Redding. They had no idea what Levi's partner had disclosed about the club, but they were going on the assumption Redding knew about Bones. Naturally, this put Clutch in a vulnerable position, but that was the whole play. Clutch was a prospect in a local club and had no idea who Redding was. At least, that was how they wanted to play it. Clutch would be armed, but then he always was. They all were.

"You watch your six, brother," Cain said as Clutch prepared to leave. "Arkham, Goose, and Deadeye will have eyes on you, and Data will be following the GPS in your truck and your cell. Your phone will give him audio so keep it with you."

"Should be no problem, especially if he buys the whole car-trouble thing. If not, the whole thing's a bust."

"He doesn't buy it, we go to plan B."

"Which is?" Clutch raised an eyebrow.

"Not for you to worry about." Cain was letting Clutch play this part, and the young man was fully aware they intended to kill his mark, but Cain wouldn't put an unpatched member unnecessarily in the know. Not because he didn't trust him, but because he would always protect him.

"Understood." The young man grinned as he finished packing. His cover story was a hunting trip where his truck broke down as he tried to head back in before the weather caught him. Clutch had secured permission with the landowner and would camp out on the property about half a mile from the house. They'd chosen a spot where he could easily monitor Redding while waiting in case the man checked. Clutch would ask Redding for a ride back to the Boneyard, then offer to buy the man a drink. If all went well, they'd get the bastard drunk, then make sure he got home. It was the man's bad luck to be renting a house fairly close to the Boneyard. Maybe a quarter mile down the road. Cain had built the bar in a remote area on purpose, since the clientele routinely did questionable business at the bar.

"Rip it up, brother," Cain said, bringing the younger man in for a hug and a solid clap to the back. "Anything seems amiss, you pull out."

"The boys got my back," Clutch said, grinning as he nodded at Arkham, Goose, and Deadeye. "Ain't no one I'd rather have watching over me."

"We'll be your guardian angels," Arkham said, rolling his eyes as if it were all some big waste of time.

Trucker knew better. So did everyone else. Arkham was a crazy son of a bitch, but he was deadly and protective of his brothers.

"Yeah, I know this one," Clutch said. "Up in the air harping about everything."

They shared a laugh, then Clutch hopped in an old Ford pick-up and left for his campsite.

"This gonna work?" Trucker asked Cain.

"If it doesn't, we'll be less subtle about the whole thing. Either way, Redding's a dead man."

"What about El Diablo?"

"One thing at a time, brother. One thing at a time."

* * *

The night before the storm was to hit, everything was on track. The boys had kept close watch on Levi Redding for four days. Clutchhad the RV parked in the perfect spot. Hidden from Redding, but giving them a great view of the little farmhouse he was renting. During that time, they noted him becoming restless. At one point, Clutch thought he might blow the joint, but Data pulled a few strings and got a flyover in the area by a friend who just happened to fly search and rescue. It took some doing, but they managed to talk them into making several rounds in the area Redding was hiding out. It was enough to drive the man back indoors after unpacking his newly acquired sedan. Also, Levi didn't appear to be one to rough it. Though he had the generator, he had no firewood and didn't use the stove at all, obviously confident that he wouldn't run out of gas. Luck was on their side.

Bones kept close eyes on the weather reports out of Jackson. So far, the storm had taken a day longer to get to them, meaning Clutch was out in the woods a day longer than anticipated. The prospect had been prepared though. Just like the good Marine he'd been before leaving the service. Anticipating the storm would hit sometime around eight that evening, he'd begun packing up camp. He'd disabled more than one system in case Redding insisted on trying to work on the truck himself. Which was difficult, given they had no idea the man's level of expertise with a vehicle. Trucker had talked Clutch through every step of the way over their secure connection. Thank God Data had the foresight to insist on the sat phones. There was no way to get a cell signal as far out as they were. Even the Boneyard had questionable service on the best of days.

Everything was going as planned, other than the small weather delay. Now, they all sat in the bar, the usual crowd creating a ruckus. Arkham reported things had gone smoothly at Redding's house and he was, indeed, bringing Clutch to the Boneyard. The show was about to begin.

"We got everyone in place?" Torpedo leaned casually against the bar, nursing a beer. Though he appeared to drink, he'd taken an empty to chase his whisky with it. In fact, he'd take a shot, then spit the contents into the bottle. They all did. It kept up the illusion they were drinking when, in fact, they were all stone-cold sober. Most of them were old hat at this trick, but it was necessary to start well before their target got there, lest the move look out of place when it counted.

"Ready and waiting," Data said. They all had earpieces and mics at their wrists to be able to communicate when necessary. Data held it all together back at the clubhouse in his command center, watching everything from a dozen different angles on a dozen different monitors. Trucker was right beside him. "Clutch and our boy should be there in five."

"Turn up the music," Torpedo said. "Get things rockin'." He raised his voice to be heard over the individual conversations. "Drinks on the house, boys!"

They did. By the time Clutch got there with Redding the place was in full swing. Every biker in the bar was drinking and having a good time. They played pool and darts, getting more and more rambunctious by the minute.

That's how things were when a smiling Clutch led Redding into the Boneyard. The man had dishwater-blond hair cut stylishly, but not flashy. He had light brown eyes and boyish good looks, but not so much he stood out in a crowd. Average height, he was a good head shorter than Clutch. In fact, there was nothing about the man that was memorable at all, if one wasn't looking for him. His disguise was perfect for his needs.

"Hey, fellas!" Clutch waved from the door. "Make room at the bar for a couple more." As expected, Redding tried to beg off, but not as hard as Trucker thought he would.

"I don't want to get in the way," Redding said. "This isn't really my scene."

"Nonsense!" Clutch clapped him on the back, deftly steering him to the bar where Pops had a beer and a shot of whisky waiting. "Everyone's friendly at the Boneyard! Ain't we, Pops?"

"Damn straight," the older man said with a grin. "Where'd you find this young'un, Clutch?"

"Man helped me out of a tight spot. Damned truck broke down. Had to leave all my gear and the fuckin' RV at the campsite. Ol' Levi here was good enough to give me a ride back to civilization."

"It was nothing," Levi said, eyeing the beer. It was obvious he wanted it, but his instinct was telling him to leave it.

"Bud and Jack," Clutch said to Pops.

"Isn't that yours?" Redding pointed to the bottle and shot glass already on the bar.

"That? Naw." Clutch waved him off. "That's yours. Pops is rarely wrong about a man's drink."

"I do like Corona," Levi said, still eyeing the bottle. "Maybe just one."

"That's the spirit!" Again, Clutch clapped him on the shoulder like the two men were best of friends. "Drink up! Gonna get cold out there tonight. You'll need a little something to warm the insides!"

"Can't argue with that." Levi squeezed the lime into the bottle and stuffed it down the neck. Then he took a healthy swig and followed it with the whisky shot on the bar. "Whoo!" He chuckled. "That's some stout stuff there!"

"It's the good stuff," Pops said proudly. "Woodford Reserve. You look like a man who likes the best."

"Well, that's damn sure close. I'll sip it next time. Savor the flavor."

"Whatever suits you. Any friend of Clutch's is a friend of mine."

"Good job, boys," Data murmured to them softly. "Give it a couple more rounds then start urgin' the locals out."

"This is really gonna work," Trucker said to himself.

"Maybe. It's not over yet." Data kept his eyes on the screens, watching Redding for any indication the man smelled a trap. So far, so good. He either didn't suspect anything or was damned good at hiding it.

Three beers later and Pops started giving more and more whiskey to Levi. The man had loosened up and was now playing pool with Clutch. The prospect was good at his role, winning one or two games before letting Levi beat him in several. There had been a couple hundred dollars on the table, and Levi was elated to have won.

"I haven't had this much fun in years," he confessed to Clutch. "Gonna haveta go bar hoppin' more often." His words were starting to slur, but he was still walking straight. It took three more beers and several more shots of whisky to remedy that, but it was definitely working. Which was when Pops brought out the moonshine.

"Here." Clutch handed Levi a shot of the clear liquid. "Peach moonshine, courtesy of the best moonshiner in Appalachia."

And so it went. Trucker watched in silence well into the night. The wind howled and everyone left the bar but the Bones crew and Levi Redding. The man who'd nearly killed Helen got drunker and drunker until he could barely stand. Still, they gave him more to drink. Clutch played his part better than anyone could have hoped, being the guy's best friend, all the while getting him closer and closer to the time the man would simply be unable to move. When he couldn't hold the glass himself, someone helped him. He drank willingly, never once trying to reject the glass held to his lips.

Finally, when he lost the ability to swallow and the liquid simply dribbled from his mouth down his chin, it was time to take him home. Clutch and Cain took on that responsibility. The snow was in full force now, blowing and drifting everywhere. By the time they got him back to the little farmhouse, the temperature was beginning to plunge, and the wind was simply *roaring*. Levi hadn't moved a muscle.

They were careful as they took Levi in the house. Stripping off his coat, they laid him on the floor. They made up the couch to look like he'd started there but had stumbled out of bed -- possibly to go to the bathroom -- and simply passed out on the floor. There was a mostly empty bottle of Woodford Reserve and a glass beside him just out of reach. Cain opened the door, and the wait was on.

They took shifts, two at a time. They all dressed in arctic gear so, while it wasn't the warmest environment imaginable, they were at least semi-comfortable. While one pair sat vigil in the house with Redding, the other four were holed up in the RV, watching the house. More than once Redding stirred. When he did, someone would give him a glass of whisky to warm him up. He always took it eagerly, even when he began shivering uncontrollably.

As the temperature dropped, Redding became more and more distressed, but couldn't quite rouse himself. Whenever he managed, a glass of whisky was shoved into his hand or to his lips. Once he stopped shivering, it was only a matter of time.

"Keep a close watch on him." Mama had entered Data's command center and helped herself to a mic and headphones. "You have to make sure he's dead before you leave. We don't need no surprises."

Another hour, and the man wasn't moving at all. His skin had gone waxy pale, and his lips had a bluish tinge to them. Clutch was on watch with Cain. Levi hadn't moved in some time. Hadn't reached for his glass or even mumbled drunkenly.

"You got a mirror handy?" Mama asked softly.

"You told me to have one, didn't you?" Cain pulled a small pocket mirror from his cargo pants and held it up to Redding's lips and nose. No steam appeared on the surface. No breath to fog the mirror. "He's officially out," Cain reported.

"Good," Data said. "I confirmed via the good Mr. Redding's email that he has this cabin rented for the rest of the month. Everything is paid in full, and there are instructions to not disturb. Fortunately, that seems to be the arrangement he had in place already."

"We've got a camera in place," Cain said. "You'll have twenty-four/seven monitoring for up to sixty days, Data. Twice what you need."

"Why not just let it go?" Clutch asked, clearly not understanding why they were going to so much trouble.

"Good question," Trucker agreed. "Why, indeed?"

"Because," Mama supplied, "just because the man seems to be dead, he can still be revived. You did this very rapidly. By doing so, you could have possibly put the brain into a hibernation-like state. If he's found by the right paramedic with the right medical control, they'll bring him to the hospital and attempt to revive him with warm fluids and such. It's even possible they could revive him, if they find him quick enough, and he could be perfectly fine. We want to make sure the bastard is good and dead. Completely frozen, as it were."

"So we leave him here." Cain stood. They'd positioned him out of direct line of sight from the door. Even if the door was open, no one could see him unless they came looking for him. Given the remoteness of the cabin and his arrangement with the owner, the chances of that were slim to none.

"Hopefully, all we'll need is a couple of days. If he makes it through this cold snap with no one finding him, his fate should be sealed. I just like to give it a little extra time. Decay or wild animals would definitely help the situation."

"Or if he freezes solid." Trucker muttered.

"Or if he freezes solid." Mama's conformation was all Cain needed.

"OK, everyone. Wrap it up. Cover our tracks and let's get the hell out of here."

Chapter Eight

One month later...

"Redding's been found," Cain whispered to Trucker. "Disemboweled and his face half-eaten."

"Coyotes?"

"Looks that way."

"What're the cops saying?" This was the day Trucker had both anticipated and dreaded. If they'd done their job right, this would all go away quietly. If not, they were going to have to do some serious working of the system.

Cain shrugged. "Drunk. Passed out at the wrong time. So far, everything is pointing to a tragic accident."

"You think she's safe?" No matter what, Trucker absolutely would not take a chance with Helen's life. If there were more people involved in this, he wanted them hunted down and disposed of sooner rather than later.

"Data has scoured every place he knows. There seem to be several people looking for Redding but no one is taking over his clients. Until today, the consensus was that he'd skipped town with the money." Cain clapped Trucker on the shoulder. "I think the danger to her's past."

"Which leaves El Diablo. We lettin' him off the hook?"

"Absolutely not." Cain answered the question without hesitation. "It's time that man was dealt with. He's hanging over us like a specter. Every time I think he's forgotten about us, he rears his ugly head."

"He's not going to let his daughter go. As long as she's with us, El Diablo will always be around, and it's not like she and Sword are going anywhere."

"No. So we've got to figure out what to do about him. Now."

"I hear you, brother."

"Now, go let your woman know the news. It's time she gives the little princess a name."

Trucker grinned. "Agreed."

He took the stairs two at a time. It was naptime for the princess, and he wanted to seduce her mother. Mama had given her the OK for sex, and Trucker was anxious to coax Helen into his bed. Once he did that, she'd start really thinking of them as a permanent couple.

As he opened the door to their suite, Trucker knew something was off. Not wrong, necessarily, but… different. He shut and locked the door, taking his time looking around the large room. A light splash came from the bathroom, and he followed the sound.

"I thought you'd never get here," Helen purred.

She relaxed in the big garden tub. The lights were dimmed, and aromatherapy candles were lit at various spots in the bathroom. Bubbles surrounded her as she lay letting the jets massage her body. The water churned with their efforts, and the bubbles lazily fizzed over her skin. All that rich auburn hair was piled on top of her head to keep it out of the water. The long line of her neck beckoned him to kiss and lick. Before he realized it, Trucker had taken a couple of steps forward.

"Holy fuck," he managed. He'd certainly seen her naked. Hell, she'd blown him in the shower more than once since that first time. But this… this was something different.

"I heard the news about Levi," Helen said softly. "Does everything seem to be going the way you wanted?"

He nodded. "Looks that way. As far as anyone is saying, Levi died of exposure related to alcohol intoxication. Data is keeping his ears open, but it looks like he and his partner were the only two in this particular scheme. If anyone else shows up or if the cops decide to take a closer look at the timeline leading up to Redding's death, we'll deal with it."

She stretched before standing. The scent of rose and lavender wafted from the water as she stood. Trucker couldn't help moving closer to inhale, wondering if her skin smelled the same.

"I know you will." Helen flashed him a grateful smile. "I can't remember if I said it before I was so nervous, but thank you. For everything. For saving my life and the life of my daughter. For taking me in and treating me like family and changing dirty diapers in the middle of the night." She stepped out of the tub, snagging a towel to wipe over her body as she walked toward him. Her hips swayed gently with every step. When she was close enough to touch him, Helen dropped the towel and laid her palm flat on his chest. Trucker felt it like a brand. "I know I have no right to stake any kind of claim on you, Trucker. But I want to." Helen looked up into his eyes. Her own eyes glistened with unshed tears.

Trucker couldn't breathe. He'd halfway expected her to cut ties with him after they killed Redding, but she'd stayed. She was here. With him. Asking to stay.

"What are you sayin', baby? And be careful. I will hold you to anything you fuckin' say."

She gave him a small smile. "I'm saying I'd like to give us a chance at a life together. That is, if you want to." When he opened his mouth to answer, she stopped him with fingers to his lips. "Before you say anything, you need to understand I'm talking about being faithful to each other. I have no idea how you bikers treat relationships, but I can't tolerate cheating."

Trucker chuckled. "Honey, that's the last thing you've got to worry about. Worry about me smothering you with protection. Two girls to take care of could drive a man crazy." He dipped his head to catch her lips with hers. "You take me on, baby, I'm all yours."

"Good." Helen gave him a dazzling smile. "Because I want you, Trucker. You're the man for me."

He picked her up, wrapping his arms around her and burying his face in her neck. For long moments, he just held her damp, naked body against his as tightly as he could. It always felt right when she was in his arms, but now more than ever. She was giving herself to him, and Trucker intended to hang on to her with both hands.

Somehow, he managed to get her dried before taking her to bed. Once he got into the thing with her, he didn't intend to leave it for several hours. Which brought up a pressing question.

"Where's the baby?"

"Mama," she breathed as she threaded her fingers through his hair and forced him to press his mouth back to hers. She was just as aggressive as he was, though she surrendered when he pushed. Helen seemed to know just what to do to drive him crazy. Just when he thought he was getting himself under control, she'd do something interesting with her tongue or squeeze his ass so that her nails dug in through his clothes, and Trucker was lost once again.

"Good. Gonna fuck you all Goddamned night, woman."

"Not if I fuck you first."

His chuckle was more than a little strained as he pressed her down into the mattress. Blanketing her body with his, Trucker relished the exquisite touch of her soft, soft skin against his. There was no way to control the thrust of his hips as he ground his cock against her through his jeans.

Helen clawed until she got his shirt off, then fumbled with the button to his jeans. She was growing increasingly frantic. So was he.

"Get my Goddamned pants down!" His voice was a growl, but his hands shook where one gripped her hip. The other held his weight off her so she could free his cock.

"Need you inside me," she whimpered. "Please, Trucker!"

"Fuck!"

Trucker couldn't think past the next few seconds. All that mattered was getting his cock in her and finding oblivion for both of them. When the tip made contact with her pussy, Trucker couldn't contain his groan of pleasure.

"So fuckin' hot," he bit out. "Scorchin' fuckin' hot!"

"Trucker!" Helen gripped his hips, digging her hails into his ass and urging him forward. She was so small beneath him, around the head of his cock. So much smaller than him. But she was perfect. Made for him.

"Don't let me hurt you, baby. Please, God, don't let me hurt you."

"You won't," she whispered. "Just get inside me. Please."

Giving himself the OK, Trucker sank into Helen's wet little pussy. They both cried out. Helen wrapped her legs around him, digging her heels in, urging him to move faster. Ever faster.

"Fuck, baby! Fuck!"

"Trucker!"

He slammed into her, holding himself still as deep as he could go. He yelled out to the ceiling as he tried to keep himself in check.

"Why'd you stop?" Her question was breathless and pleading. "I need you to fuck me hard!"

"I intend to fuck the shit outta you, baby. But I'm not rushing this."

"We've got all fucking night!" she wailed. "Don't stop now!"

"Goddamn it, Helen!"

There was no help for it. Trucker started fucking her again, this time in earnest. Being inside her body was a paradise like no other, the pleasure so intense he lost his mind.

Wrapping his arms tightly around her, Trucker pulled her to him with every thrust. Helen clung to him, their bodies growing damp with sweat.

"Come on my cock, baby," he urged, growling in her ear. "Do it. Milk my come from me."

"TRUCKER!" She screamed his name, arching her back and writhing as she came. He held her as she writhed in his arms, only letting himself go when the spasms started lessening around his dick. When he came inside her, he did so with a deafening bellow.

It was long moments before either of them could speak. Trucker stayed buried inside her, lying on top of her and savoring the feel of her in his arms. He'd held her many times over the weeks she'd been with him. But not like this. Not with his dick buried to the balls inside her, his come leaking from her tight pussy.

Finally, because he didn't want to crush her, Trucker rolled them to their sides. Helen still clung to him, kissing and sucking his neck and chest as she lay there. He nuzzled her head, kissing her hair and nosing his way through the thick mass where it had come loose during their lovemaking until he found her temple with his lips.

"I don't want to move," he confessed, "but I need to clean us up." Reluctantly, he extracted himself from her body. "Don't move. I'll be right back."

He gave himself a once-over in the bathroom before bringing a warm washcloth to clean Helen. She'd turned over on her back and stretched languidly. She'd spread her legs and bent them at the knees, opening herself to him. As he cleaned her, Trucker was mesmerized at the sight of her trimmed pussy. Dark auburn curls a couple shades darker than her hair beckoned him. Her pussy lips were swollen and red with his use of her, so he knew he had to be careful, but he wanted another taste of her. Before he thought about it much, he dipped his head and found her clit with his tongue.

"Oh! Ohhh..." He'd caught her off guard with that little trick, but, honestly, he wasn't letting a little thing like his own come get in the way of what he wanted. Besides, it was bound to happen sooner or later. Might as well get it over with.

"Gonna make you come again before we rest," he murmured around her clit. "Then gonna fuck you again. You good with that?"

"Oh, yeah! I'm definitely good with that." She chuckled. It sounded a little strained, but she didn't try to push him away or close her legs. If anything, she opened herself up even more. "Feels so fucking good!"

Trucker continued to lick and flick her clit, sucking the little bud between his lips and tugging until she was once again squirming beneath him. "That's it, baby. You gonna come for me?"

"I'm so close," she gasped. "So fucking close!"

Trucker inserted two thick fingers inside her, pumping her little cunt like he was fucking her. Again, she cried out, but he was careful not to push her over the edge. Not yet. "Wanted this too fuckin' long," he muttered. "You at my mercy, beggin' me for release."

"Please! Oh, God! Please!"

He removed his fingers from her only to swipe his hand through her pussy, wetting his fingers with her honey before sinking them back inside her. Carefully, watching her reaction even as he continued to tongue her clit, he slipped his little finger between her cheeks and past the rim of her ass. Instantly, Helen raised herself on her elbows, gasping in surprise. Trucker continued to work both her holes with slow, steady strokes.

"How's that, my wicked little girl?"

"Oh, you're a bad boy," she purred. "Fuck!"

"Oh, I'm gonna fuck you all right. Gonna fuck your mouth, your pussy, and, when I get you ready, I'm gonna fuck this sweet little ass. Then I'm never letting you go. You'll be mine for as long as we both live."

With those promises, Trucker eased another finger into her ass, stretching her just a little. Helen screamed, bearing down on him as her orgasm washed over her with alarming intensity. Trucker watched as her whole body blushed right before his eyes. The veins stood out at her temples as she screamed her pleasure. Never had he seen a woman have such a powerful orgasm. Never had he felt anything remotely close to the tight vise her body had on his fingers. In that moment, he'd have given anything to have his cock in her ass. She'd probably squeeze the life right out of him.

Before she could completely come down, he crawled up her body and slipped inside her little cunt once again, fucking her in long, hard, demanding strokes until he could feel her breaths coming in little gasps as she began to climb that mountain once again. This time, when she crested, she took him with her into oblivion. Trucker came so hard his vision blurred, and he saw stars around the edges. Both of them shouted their pleasure as he exploded inside her once again.

This time, he had no idea how he was going to manage to get to the bathroom to clean them both. Thank God he'd left the washcloth on the bedside table. He rolled off her and gently washed his seed from her before wiping his dick and tossing the soiled cloth into the bathroom.

Trucker pulled Helen into his arms, clasping her to him tightly. Her hand rested on his chest and her warm breath fanned over his skin. It was contentment unlike anything in his experience. It was… love.

They lay like that so long, Trucker thought she'd drifted to sleep, but then she stirred. "I found out your name," she said softly. "It's William. Isn't it?"

He kissed her forehead. "Yeah. William Norvac. Data tell you?"

"I did some digging on my own," she teased, nipping his chest. "You're an engineer."

"I am. Got a degree from MIT, for all the good it does me."

"Why'd you join the Marines after you graduated? You could have worked anywhere in the world you wanted."

"True." He nodded. "But that wasn't my callin'. I was born to be a soldier. I used my talents to serve my country. I met Cain in the service and been followin' him ever since."

"I've been thinking, and I've come up with a name for the baby," she said, throwing Trucker. She was nervous, he could tell. Probably why she changed the subject so abruptly.

"Have you then. Well..." He sifted his hands through her hair, trying to soothe her. "Let's hear it."

"I thought I'd name her Willa." She peeked up at him. "After the man I'd like to be her father figure."

Trucker stilled. His heart pounded. God, he couldn't bungle this! "Willa, huh."

"Yeah." She was practically holding her breath. Trucker needed to speak, but couldn't for the lump in his throat. If she didn't mean what he thought she meant, he was getting ready to make an ass out of himself.

"Willa sounds an awful lot like William. Don't suppose you had another William in mind, did you?"

"Um, no." Her voice was soft. Hesitant. "I was hoping you'd take on the job. You know. Unless Cain keeps you too busy in Bones."

"I think I can work around anything Cain needs from me." He urged her to look at him, pinching her chin with his thumb and forefinger. When she met his gaze with her wide-eyed green one, Trucker smiled at her. "It would be my sincerest honor to be a father to her, Helen. Just don't expect her to date until she's at least forty. You remember that, and we'll be all good."

Helen giggled, but let out a harsh breath. "Oh, Trucker!" She wrapped her arms around him, and he felt her hot tears on his bare flesh.

"Shh, baby," he soothed. "That's supposed to make you happy."

"I am happy! So very happy!"

"So, I have a question for you, now."

"OK."

Trucker let go of her long enough to roll over and fumble in the nightstand drawer. Fishing out a tiny box, he opened it and handed it to her. Inside was a ring set of diamonds and dark blue sapphires. The main stone in the engagement ring was the blue sapphire. On either side, diamonds were set into a braided pattern with smaller sapphires in the gathers of the braid. The wedding band was the same only without the larger stone in the center. They were stunning.

"When did you get this?" Helen breathed, her gaze transfixed on the ring.

"Ordered it made right after the storm broke. Wanted to have it ready when you were ready."

She lifted her head and tears glistened on her lashes, shaming the diamonds in her ring. "How'd you know I was ready?"

"Well, naming your daughter after me wasn't a subtle clue."

A laugh burst from her, a short bark of amusement before she sniffled. For long, long moments, she just looked at him. She didn't have to say anything. Trucker could see the love shining in her eyes.

"I love you, Trucker. I think I have from the moment you picked me up and carried me so carefully out of that RV."

"Hell, I lost my heart the first moment I laid eyes on you. You scared me to death, but I couldn't get you out of my heart. Didn't want to."

He lowered his head and kissed her, sweeping his tongue inside her mouth to dance with hers. "I love you so fuckin' much, Helen."

Her fingers tugged at his hair, fisting there and holding him close to her. "Love you, too," she said between kisses.

Then, they proceeded to show each other exactly how much.

Vicious (Salvation's Bane MC 1)
Marteeka Karland

Lucrecia: All I have in the world is my sister Mae. We were adrift, on our own until a guy from Black Reign, one of Lake Worth's most infamous MCs, spotted us and took us in. Rycks isn't cruel, but he's hard on us. We have to earn our keep, but then everyone does. Me? I dance for the club. I get a secret thrill from it -- until Mae is kidnapped by enemies of Black Reign, and Rycks sends me to Palm Beach -- straight into the hands of Salvation's Bane.

Vicious: It all started when some MFer stole my f-n pizza and two cans of beer. I went looking for the SOB. What I found was a raven-haired spitfire too sexy for my own good. Her sister's in trouble, and wouldn't you know it that bastard El Diablo's at the very center of yet more trouble. It's his club Mae's been taken from. His club Lucy was sent away from. Now, we have to get Mae back. Because I might be falling for the little dancer in my care. Not that I'll ever admit it. We'll have to call out all the stops for this. Bones. Shadow Demons. Hell, even Black Reign. If we're going to rescue Mae, nothing is out of bounds. But busting her out of some rich banker's estate will be a piece of cake. No worries.

Yeah. Right...

Chapter One

"God fuckin' damn it! That fuckin' pizza box had my fuckin' name on it! Who the fuck ate my fuckin' pizza?"

"My, Vicious, aren't we a grumpy bear." Havoc, vice president of Salvation's Bane MC, was a huge smartass, but Vicious put up with him because he was also one of the best men he'd ever served with. Both as a SEAL and as an MC brother.

"I want my Goddamned pizza!" He *was* grumpy. That pizza had been the best fucking pizza he'd ever eaten, and he'd been looking forward to eating the rest for breakfast. "What the Goddamned fuck?"

"Beats the fuck outta me. Maybe it was Mercedes. Looks like she finally cleaned up the fuckin' kitchen."

Vicious snorted. "Mercedes never did this good a job. Girl needs to leave but is either too stubborn or too stupid to take the hint." He rubbed the back of his neck, the fine hairs there prickling a subtle warning. Why, he didn't know, but something didn't seem right to him.

"True." Havoc flashed him a lecherous grin. "But, Goddamn, the girl has a sweet pussy." When Vicious gave him an exasperated look, Havoc added, "What? Tell me I'm wrong." When he opened his mouth to tell Havoc to go to hell, the man held up a hand. "Keep in mind you're the fuckin' chaplain. Don't that mean you ain't supposed to lie? Cause if you say you didn't have her, or that her pussy ain't sweet, I'll call you a Goddamned liar."

"Fine. Fucker."

"So? Do you agree or not?"

He couldn't help it. Vicious chuckled, scrubbing his hand over his face. "Yeah. The girl has a sweet fuckin' pussy. Knows how to use it too."

They both laughed.

"Don't think I'm letting this go, brother," Vicious said. "I'm findin' out who stole my fuckin' pizza and I'm gonna nail someone's balls to the fuckin' wall."

"So, let's talk about Mercedes."

"I just won a fuckin' million dollars, you cocksucker." Vicious tried to snarl at Havoc, but it only came out a sigh.

"Oh? How's that?"

"I bet myself a mil that was why you brought up Mercedes' name in the first Goddamned place. What the fuck did she do now?"

Havoc raised his hand in surrender. "Not a fuckin' thing, brother. Just wondering where we stood with her. You know as well as I do -- great lay aside -- the girl don't belong here. She needs to go back to wherever she came from before she gets hurt."

"I know. Thought assigning her stuff to do, outside of fuckin', would help her realize just how much she wasn't ready for this, but I think she's got it in her head she's gonna be Thorn's ol' lady. You know. Get some clout in the club and have the girls all submitting to her every whim."

Havoc shook his head. "Yeah. Figured. Girl ain't smart enough to figure out a brother doesn't take an ol' lady from the club girl population, especially if everyone in the fuckin' club has already screwed her."

"She's a spoiled little rich girl, trying to thwart her daddy or some shit. I'd hoped she'd leave on her own but I'm afraid I'm gonna have to get Thorn to go with me and help her come to the decision."

"Well, I ain't seen her in a couple days. Maybe she already bailed."

"Maybe. I'll check her room in a while. You know. Soon as I find the motherfuckin' cocksuckin' son of a bitch who stole my fuckin' pizza."

Havoc snickered then pushed off the counter to leave. "Let me know what you decide. I'll tell the guys to back off for a while."

Vicious waved Havoc on, not sparing him a glance as he continued to stare into the fridge like the stupid pizza would just appear in front of him. He wished it would cause it was a seriously good pie. Which was when he noticed two of the six beers he'd put in the fridge next to the pizza were also gone. Someone was getting a beatdown like never before.

"Mother fuck," he bit out. "Mother Goddamned *fuck*."

He stalked into the common room. It was a perfect day for riding, so it didn't surprise him no one was there. Red, the road captain, had organized a ride for that evening, but, true to form, no one wanted to wait that long. Likely, the whole club had taken off in pairs for a little free time on the road.

With a growl he clenched his fists. No use getting angry right now. His wrath would be wasted with everyone gone. Might as well go check Mercedes's room. If the girl was gone, he'd need to make sure it was cleaned out and any personal belongings she left behind bagged and stored in case she came back for them. He hoped she was in her room because he was dying to confront someone. While protocol demanded Thorn be with him if he evicted a non-club inhabitant, it wasn't strictly necessary. His job was to see to the wellbeing of the club and anyone living with them.

Mercedes's behavior was self-destructive. She needed to go home.

He stomped up the stairs. Club members were on the first floor. Women not ol' ladies were on the second floor in the middle rooms. Officers took the rooms on the outside, so the women were protected on both sides and below. Mercedes was no exception. In fact, Vicious had been careful to put her as close to the center as he could because he'd known sooner or later someone would come looking for her, and he wanted to be able to tell the girl's father she'd been as protected as any woman in their club. Of course, he'd neglect to mention she'd fucked nearly every single patched member in Salvation's Bane. Cause, yeah. No.

He was surprised to find the door wide open and stripped bare of anything other than the furniture. He sighed. Well, it was one less thing he had to deal with.

Again, that prickly sensation on the back of his neck had him rubbing it before scrubbing a hand through his hair. His years as a SEAL had him refusing to ignore the feeling. It had saved his life more than once, but what the fuck? Danger? In his own clubhouse? No fucking way.

Still, he gave the room a visual once-over. The longer he stood there, the louder his senses pinged. He wished he had a better idea of how the room should be, but with the recent departure of its occupant, all he had to go on was immediate visual clues. He moved around the room slowly, looking at the windows, the bathroom and windows there, the walls, and the ceiling. He was about to chalk it up to him being a paranoid son of a bitch when there was a muffled sneeze from the bathroom.

"What the fuck?" His muttered question seemed loud but was met with silence. Once again, Vicious checked the bathroom. Nothing. It wasn't exactly like there were a ton of places to hide. The place was pretty small. Wide enough for the bathtub/shower at the far end, the toilet beside the tub, and the sink beside the toilet. The window was in front of the sink with a small, wall-mounted cabinet for towels and washcloths beside the window. The only other closed-in space was the vanity under the sink.

Before he thought about it, Vicious opened the door under the sink and shut it again. Did a double take. He opened the cabinet door again to find a small girl tucked in the limited space, folded with her knees against her chest. Her eyes were enormous. A vibrant gold framed with coal-black lashes. Jet-black hair tumbled around her in tight curls. Cutoff shorts and a black tank revealed snow-white skin. Skin that looked like it had never seen the sun a single day in her life.

"What the everlastin' fuck?" Vicious tried not to raise his voice too much. This girl didn't look like she could take the shock of a six-foot-seven, three-hundred-pound man roaring at her. She looked like it would be nothing for him to break her in half. "Get your ass outta there, young lady!" Great. Now he sounded like an old man.

The girl hesitated until he tilted his head, giving her his best *so help me...* expression. Then she squeaked her distress as she tumbled out of the cramped space to stand in front of him. Good thing he was between her and the door, because he was certain she'd have tried to make a run for it otherwise.

"Wanna tell me what the fuck you're doin' in here?" That was when he noticed two empty beer bottles and a mostly eaten slice of pizza lying in her little hiding place. Upon further inspection, the girl had pizza sauce in the corner of her lips and on her chin.

"You little thief!" He wasn't really mad. Kid looked like she was starving. Didn't mean he could let her transgression go unpunished.

"Am not," she said defiantly, her chin going up a notch. "I cleaned that hell hole you call a kitchen as payment. It was worth a whole pizza and a six pack. You're lucky I settled for what was left of that pizza and only two beers." The second her mouth was closed, she let out a very impressive and unladylike belch. Apparently, he'd interrupted her meal, and the beer hadn't yet settled. A pink flush swept up her neck to her face. Her eyes watered, and she turned her head away from him instead of meeting his gaze boldly as she had just moments before. Little thing had a fierce pride.

Vicious chose to ignore her embarrassment, not wanting her uncomfortable with something silly. Besides, seeing her so miserable did something to his chest. He rubbed it absently as he spoke. "Nobody asked you to clean the kitchen. People here have tasks, and that was supposed to be someone else's job."

"Well, whoever it was wasn't doing so hot. You should be thanking me instead of giving me shit."

"That so?"

"Yeah. It is."

"What's your name, girl?"

She put her chin up, her face and neck still a bright red. "Ain't none of your business."

"It is when you steal my pizza and my beer, then hole up in my house."

"Oh, please," she scoffed. "There are so many people here, you never noticed me."

He raised an eyebrow. "You think so?"

"None of you had a clue I was here."

"How long you been holed up?"

"Again. Ain't none of your business."

Vicious still wasn't mad or even annoyed at her presence. Deep down, he thought more than one of them had thought something was amiss but hadn't really paid much attention. There had never been anything overt out of place or anything. Just the occasional missing food. Sometimes, the girls had bickered back and forth over missing clothing items, but everything had always turned up in a few days. Also, things had been considerably cleaner in the past couple weeks. He narrowed his eyes at her.

"You've been here two and a half weeks, haven't you?"

Her eyes widened before she masked her expression with a shrug as she looked away. "More or less."

Vicious looked at her. Really looked at her. "Where's your home?" When she stubbornly remained silent, he sighed. "You can't stay here, girl. This is no place for the likes of you." It wasn't. She was too young and too innocent looking to survive in their world. The women would eat her alive. The men… Well. They'd eat her alive. She just couldn't stay here. Unbidden, the thought of him beating the shit out of Beast, the enforcer and resident playboy, sprang into his mind. If the man so much as touched a hair on this girl's head…

Where the fuck had that thought come from? Hell, was she even eighteen? She didn't look it.

"Why not? You never knew I was anywhere on the grounds. I'm not in the way at all!"

"'Cause we don't work that way. And you would never fit in." The second the words were out of his mouth, Vicious wanted to take them back. They were true, but the crestfallen look on her face made him wince.

"Fine." She said, turning to snag the last of the pizza she'd dropped, taking a huge bite so all that was left was the crust. Two bites later, even that was gone. She pushed past Vicious out of the bathroom, swiping her forearm across her mouth and wiping her hands on her shirt as she went.

As she marched across the bedroom to the door, Vicious got a good look at her from the back. A really good look. Her tank top was cropped and showed off her midriff and those cutoff shorts revealed miles of milky white legs. Canvas shoes were on her little feet. What caused him to suck in a breath and nearly fall to his knees to worship her in adoration was that ass. Until that moment, Vicious had been positive she was no more than a teenager. She might not be much older, but, Goddamn, no kid could possibly have an ass like hers. It was rounded and supple looking, but firm. He could tell because it hardly moved as she stalked away from him. The shorts she wore were a pale blue with frayed ends, not quite Daisy Dukes, but definitely not hiding much of what they so lovingly hugged. He thought he could just make out the outline of a thong.

"Stop," he said in his most commanding voice.

She huffed in exasperation. "Can you not make up your freaking mind?"

"You're in my house, girl. I don't have to make up my mind."

"Well, I can't very well leave if you don't pick a plan and stick to it. Either I stay or I go. Makes no difference to me."

She shrugged, but Vicious could tell it did matter. "I kick you out, where you goin'?"

"God!" she snapped as she turned around, obviously exasperated with him beyond her endurance. "You're right. I'm trespassing." She flung her arms out. "I'll leave, and you won't have to worry about me."

"You see, that's where you're wrong." He crossed his arms over his chest. "I should not 'a been such an ass. I'm willin' to bet you don't have anywhere to go, or you wouldn't be here."

She rolled her eyes. "I should've known you'd be a bastard. He said you would be. Wanted me to go to Kentucky, but I can't leave my sister here alone."

"Who? Who told you I was a bastard?"

The girl looked away, for the first time looking completely vulnerable. "Nobody."

Vicious took the three steps separating them and grabbed her upper arms, forcing her to look up at him. He might as well have sunk to his knees in front of her. Up close, she was perfection. The porcelain skin of her face was framed by jet-black curls in haphazard rings. Her eyebrows were dark slashes over her eyes. And those eyes… a mesmerizing gold. Black lashes made them stand out even more. She was, in a word, exquisite. A delicate rose-and-honeysuckle scent seemed to cling to her. Those eyes of hers were at once innocent yet had seen too much. Been through too much. Looking into their depths, he could see she fully expected him to hurt her in some way.

Closing his eyes and taking a deep breath, Vicious calmed himself. The last thing he wanted to do was make her fear for her safety. He should, but he couldn't. If he did, she'd probably leave, and he knew the same as he knew his own name she had no one. No place to go.

"Where in Kentucky were you supposed to go?"

"Does it matter?"

"Yes. Because I have a feeling you were supposed to go to a little place called Somerset. A club called Bones. Am I right?" He could tell by the way those exotic eyes widened he was.

"How'd you know?"

"When you refused to leave your sister, did he tell you to come to us?" She nodded. "Bones is our sister club. Little far apart, but it works for us. Now, tell me who it was who told you to come here. Then I want you to tell me why."

She sighed, obviously realizing she'd lost this round. "Doesn't matter anyway," she muttered. "His name is El Diablo. He's president of Black Reign in Lake Worth. He and Rycks told me, if I wanted to live, I'd go to Bones. When I refused to leave Florida without my sister, he told me to come to Salvation's Bane. He said I might talk you into helping me. I had no intention of asking anyone for help, but I decided holing up in an MC clubhouse would be safer than hiding on my own."

"Where's your sister?"

"She was taken by enemies of Black Reign. More accurately, by enemies of El Diablo and the men he brought with him to Black Reign. Apparently, she was supposed to be leverage. While El Diablo doesn't much care, Rycks apparently does."

"Never thought it would make a difference to El Diablo if one of his officers did care. He's not exactly the compassionate soul."

"No. He's not. He's the scariest man I've ever met. But he's fiercely loyal to his inner circle, and apparently Rycks wants my sister back."

"She his woman?" This was going to get complicated.

"No. But I think he wants her to be. If not that, I have no idea. He's hell-bent on getting her back, and they wanted me out of the way."

"Afraid you'd get hurt?"

She shrugged. "No. I was just in the way. A liability, I guess."

Vicious was silent a long time, mulling this over. Even if he could convince Thorn to help this girl find her sister, if Black Reign had a claim to her, she'd never be able to leave their compound. Where did that leave her?

"I need your name. Can't do nothing without knowing that."

"Lucrecia Stephens. My sister's name is Mae."

He blinked. "Your name's a fuckin' mouthful."

"Most everyone calls me Lucy." She shrugged, looking for all the world like she could care less he'd just insulted her. Vicious knew better. He could see hurt in her expressive eyes.

"Sorry," he muttered. "It's an unusual name." He tilted his head, using the opportunity to check her out once more. "I think it suits you."

"Cause I'm a freak?" The little laugh she gave him was anything but humorous. "Never liked it, but I guess it does suit me."

"Look at me," he snapped. Just like he knew she would, her gaze snapped to his tone of authority. "I was an ass. There's nothing wrong with you other than you ate my fuckin' pizza and drank my fuckin' beer."

She managed a small giggle, which warmed Vicious's chest more than was good for him. He was so fucked.

"You know why they have your sister?" He needed to get the subject back on track.

"From what I could gather, El Diablo has something these guys want. He's not giving it to them, and they've threatened to start sending Mae back in pieces." There was a little quiver to her voice and her lower lip trembled slightly, but she quickly swallowed and gritted her teeth.

"Bloody hell." Vicious pulled out his phone and called Thorn. His president answered on the first ring. "We may have a situation."

"Don't we always." Thorn sounded bored, but Vicious knew his brother well enough to know that was his calm before the storm.

"We have a stowaway. And she's linked to Black Reign."

There was a long pause, then a heavy sigh. "It was bound to happen sooner or later. She OK?"

"Fine. I'd like to call Data with Bones. Put him on it. See if he can dig up something we can't find. Said Black Reign sent her here. Anyone call you with the details?"

"No. It's past fuckin' time to do something about this fucker El Diablo. If he's sendin' trouble, the least the bastard could do is give me a heads up." Thorn heaved a sigh into the phone. "Good idea to get Bones involved. Even better, see if he can get Sword to find out what's going on. Being El Diablo's son-in-law ought to have some perks."

Vicious ended the call, then gave Lucrecia his most intimidating stare. "You got anything else in here?" She shook her head. "Come with me."

"Where're we going?"

"To put you in a room where you can sleep somewhere other than under the fuckin' sink."

Chapter Two

Lucrecia knew she was in a world of trouble. The men of Black Reign hadn't been unkind, but it had been clear they cared more about protecting whatever their enemies wanted than anyone in the clubhouse. She and Mae had only been with them a couple of weeks. The enforcer, Rycks, had allowed them to stay. Lucrecia had no idea why. The man seemed to hate everyone. The only people he showed respect to were El Diablo and a man they called El Segador. The Reaper.

Rycks sought out Mae every day and taunted her mercilessly. He wasn't exactly mean, but he let her know she didn't belong there. Only seventeen, Mae tried to look and dress older than she was because she was a dancer. She and Lucrecia both had made more money exotic dancing than either had first thought possible. It hadn't bought them a home, but it had helped pay off their father's debts. She'd finally paid the guy off and had hoped to start saving for a home for her and Mae. Rycks had no idea how old she or Mae were. None of them did. At first.

Rycks had spotted them in the club one night and strong-armed Lucy and Mae into a private performance for Black Reign that promised to pay double what they could have made at the club. At first, Lucrecia refused. There was no way either of them was prostituting herself. At least, Mae wasn't going to. Lucrecia would do what she had to in order to protect her little sister. But, given the attention Rycks was giving Mae, Lucrecia doubted he would let her substitute for Mae.

Finally, Mae talked Lucy into it. It would finish their payments to Tubs, the mob guy her dad owed.

Being out from under that shadow was more of a relief than Lucy had been willing to admit at the time. She only agreed to going with Rycks with the understanding neither of them was turning tricks. It was an exotic dance only. Rycks had hastily agreed and taken them to the Black Reign clubhouse. Where he'd kept them. Every time Lucrecia mentioned leaving, Rycks would intimidate her into staying. He didn't lay a hand on Mae the whole time they were there. Didn't even allow her to fully strip. In fact, he'd insisted she dance for him the way she wanted to dance, to Mae's delight. She'd studied ballet and contemporary dance and readily gave performances to anyone who wanted to watch. Rycks had encouraged her to dance regularly. Soon, she had a crowd gathering the second she entered the common room. The pay had been outstanding. She'd danced in skimpy outfits, but had never completely stripped, which relieved Lucy to no end.

Lucrecia had danced every night for the club. An hour. Two if they had a party with other clubs. A few men -- and women -- had pawed her, but no worse than any other night at work. More than one had tried to coax her into their beds. When she'd said no, they'd looked crestfallen, but had only tipped her extra and grinned. They were a rowdy bunch, but pleasant enough.

Though there were several club girls, none of them seemed to be claimed by any one man. No one latched on to any single man, and the men simply took what was offered. All but two young women.

Serilda and Winter were sisters who kept mostly to themselves. Sometimes Rycks would coax them out into the common room if there was a less rambunctious gathering of the club. They were timid and anti-social, but Lucrecia could see they wanted to be part of the group. They just didn't seem to know how. Though Rycks had taken on the role of protector, the rest of the club took special care to make sure the two women felt safe. None of them approached the girls too suddenly and they never touched them. They were always kind and took care to include them if they could, but it was obvious they weren't ready to join normal society for whatever reason. Had the men treated them differently than what Lucy had observed, she'd have done everything she could to get them out. Instead, the girls looked to Rycks and a few other members of the club as if they were the last line of defense between them and the rest of the world.

Everything changed when Mae had been taken. Every single one of them to the man had turned deadly. Serilda and Winter had been taken away with four of the club members sent to guard them. The rest had prepared for war. She could see it in their eyes. When they looked at her, that is. Mostly they avoided her, as if she were a distraction.

That was when El Diablo and Rycks had insisted she leave. They'd said they had no place for her anymore, and they'd do their best to find her sister and gave Lucy a bus ticket to Somerset, Kentucky. When she'd refused, not wanting to leave without Mae, Rycks had rolled his eyes, dumped her in a pick-up truck, and taken her to Palm Beach. He'd handed her written instructions on how to find the Salvation's Bane clubhouse. Told her to get in and stay there. As long as she was with either Salvation's Bane or Bones, she'd be safe.

Yeah, the jury was still out on that one.

Instead of approaching the club, she'd watched a couple of days, camping in an abandoned shop.

Finally, she'd found her way in. The woman who'd recently left the club had a room she barely stayed in. Apparently, she went from man to man in the club. Not Lucy's taste, but to each her own. Lucy had stayed hidden in Mercedes's room. Mostly, she'd slept in the closet, but occasionally, she'd had to find other alternatives. Which is how she'd ended up under the sink. Cramped, but she was small.

Her attention was drawn back to Vicious when he stopped in front of a door and opened it.

"Here," he growled. Mr. Personality he was not. "Inside until we decide what the fuck to do with you."

Had he not been such an asshole, Lucy would have gravitated toward him. It wasn't that he was handsome -- at least, not in the conventional way. Tattoos covered him wherever there was skin except for his face. Scars crisscrossed over him at random. Some looked like knife wounds, others more like bullet wounds. But, hell, she wasn't a medical person. All she knew was this man was a warrior.

"How about I just leave. You don't have to worry about it then."

"Unless you're a plant by El Diablo."

"Ouch." She mock-winced. "You really know how to hit a girl where it hurts."

"I do, but I don't make a habit of it. Unless she betrays my brothers." His dark eyes held death. That much was certain. She had no idea how he'd come by the name Vicious, but she could definitely tell he had a mean streak.

"Look, I told you everything I know. El Diablo did send me, but not to spy or anything. He just wanted me out of the way."

"Then why not just kick you out? Why send you to Bones or here?"

"I don't know. I think it was because of Rycks. And before you ask, I have no idea what his motivations are. He's just... protective. At least, he is with Mae."

"Stay here."

"Wait!" He'd turned to go, but Lucy didn't like not knowing where she was or what to expect. She'd been there two weeks, but she hadn't explored. Sure, she'd scavenged the girls' clothing, but it had all been in the laundry room. Sitting there. Waiting for someone to wash. She had, then, helped herself. She'd always returned anything she'd borrowed to the dirty pile. The only room she'd ventured into had been Mercedes's. The woman was never there, so why not? Though she'd been in the clubhouse, she'd kept to herself, only venturing out when the club as a collective was gone. Which happened only three times a week.

"Whose room am I in? I don't want someone thinking I broke in or some shit."

He leveled a look at her. Now, she already knew Vicious could be a scary man. She'd seen it in the way he looked at her in the beginning. She'd heard him with his brothers more than once over the days she'd been here, but she'd never seen this particular look in those fathomless dark eyes. "Mine."

She sucked in a breath and backed up one defensive step. There was something in his gaze. He let it travel over her from top to bottom. Lucy was almost certain it was a reflex on his part. As if sizing up potential prey. That look was at once hot and possessive. Lucy had seen the possessive looks Rycks gave Mae, but they were nothing like this. Vicious looked... primal. Even more than that. This was the side she'd always expected to see from the men she'd been around since Rycks had taken her and Mae in months earlier. Now, she knew she was right to fear it.

"I'm not sure that's a good idea."

"Don't much care about your opinion. It's my decision. You're staying here until Thorn gives me further instruction."

"Right. He tells you to let me go, you gonna do it?"

He smirked at her. "Baby, he ain't gonna tell me to let you go."

"You can't know that!" Lucy clenched her fists at her side, knowing deep down in her gut that, if she didn't get out of here now, this man -- Vicious -- would never let her leave. How she knew it, she couldn't say. But it was there between them. In the air around them.

"I can. I do. You're here until I say otherwise."

"I thought Thorn was the president."

Vicious shrugged. "He is. But all it takes is one of us to suggest there might be reason for him to rethink a decision, especially one like this. Holding you a few days while we look into Black Reign isn't unreasonable. Even knowing that, I know my president. Thorn ain't lettin' you go until he's satisfied you're not here for more sinister reasons." He grinned. "You keep that sweet little ass parked right here, baby. I'll send up food and be back later."

* * *

Vicious tried his best to take care of business as usual. He'd done as he promised and had food delivered and had one of the prospects take it to her. He had no idea what she liked or disliked, so he played it safe with a good-quality pizza. His has been pepperoni, so he'd gotten her the same. After that, he'd put her out of his mind. There were other things for him to worry about.

Like fucking El Diablo. The man was up to something. No way would a man like him back down from anything. It wouldn't matter who his enemies had taken. That man wouldn't budge. He might fight back, might attack, but if push came to shove, he'd leave that girl in the tender hands of her captors to protect whatever they wanted. Not necessarily because it was valuable, but because it was *his*. If he traded for the girl, it would show weakness. They'd have something on El Diablo and Black Reign they could exploit, and they would never stop. No. If Mae were going to be rescued, it wouldn't be by Black Reign. The question was, could Vicious convince Thorn to get involved?

And why the fuck was he even considering asking Thorn in the first Goddamned place?

"Tell me, Vicious." Thorn and Havoc approached him. Which meant it was on. His brothers were taking this very seriously.

"Our stowaway was sent here by El Diablo's man, Rycks. Apparently, he tried to send her to Bones, but the girl refused to leave her sister behind. And that's where the problem is."

"Why is it always a sister or brother or mother?" Havoc mused. He was genuinely giving the question thought.

"Really, Havoc? That's what you're focused on?" Vicious loved his levelheaded brother, but the man was too… logical sometimes. He was an academic genius, and sometimes it took his thought process places they didn't have the time or inclination to share.

Havoc shrugged. "Just pointing it out."

"No, you weren't. You were thinking of all the times we've been pulled into a problem because of someone's family. Did it ever occur to you it's just coincidence? Or maybe that people just care about family?"

"Vicious," Thorn snapped. "Focus on the fuckin' problem, will you?"

When Havoc smirked, Vicious realized his mistake. Havoc had intentionally baited him, and he'd swallowed it hook, line, and sinker. He promptly flipped off his brother.

"Data from Bones is working on finding out exactly who we're dealing with, but it looks like El Diablo has some mean mother fuckers on him."

"Like that was unexpected," Havoc muttered.

"Not like you might think. Once I understood, it surprised the fuck outta me." Vicious meant it too. "The last thing I expected when dealing with a man like El Diablo was to trace trouble back to some swanky investment banker, but that's exactly where Data ended up."

"*Insider trading*? Are you fucking kiddin' me?" Havoc's eyes were wide, and he looked like he was about to break out in peals of laughter. "Knew from the beginnin' that bastard wasn't a hard ass. He's playing at being rough. Probably to scare his white-collar buddies to keep 'em in line. Oh, this is rich!"

"Don't kid yourself, Havoc. Man's still dangerous as fuck." Thorn stroked his beard with one hand, pondering what Vicious was telling him. "You said the trail ended there. Who's in the middle?"

It was Vicious's turn to smirk at Havoc. "I didn't say it ended there, just that Data traced him back there. Investment banker is the person in the middle of it all. Apparently, a company called Rush Developments is owned by someone who knows someone who works for someone else who uses Independent Banking who just happens to be where this investment banker works. Rush Developments is a tech company on the rise, directly competing with a company you might recognize. Ever hear of Argent Tech?"

"Well, fuck me raw," Havoc said. "Why do I get the feeling there is something about El Diablo we're missing?"

"Because we are. Data is bringing in Giovanni Romano from Shadow Demons. They own Argent Tech, and it sounds like they need to be brought up to speed."

"What are the odds El Diablo ended up where he is, as president of Black Reign? A club in our backyard when we're a sister club to Bones, and Shadow Demons use Cain's company, ExFil, for security on a regular basis?" Thorn was on the same path Vicious was.

"Don't believe in coincidences," Vicious said. "Especially not ones that big."

"He wanted all of us as a buffer between him and whomever is on the other side of that investment banker." Thorn led the way to the basement where they usually held church. Though this wasn't a formal meeting involving all the club members, they needed someplace they could talk and plan without being disturbed. "So, if Rush Developments is where it starts, El Diablo is the go-to guy, who's on the other end? Who are we really fighting here?"

"That's the six-million-dollar question," Vicious answered. "He's working on it. I'm betting Data and Giovanni can put it all together. Just give them time."

"In the meantime, what do we do about your girl?" Thorn raised an eyebrow at Vicious. Try as he might, Vicious couldn't hold his president's gaze when he answered him.

"She ain't my girl. I just found her, brother."

"Right," Thorn said, obviously not buying it. Havoc didn't even try to hide his snort.

"Hey, I just found her. Don't mean I'm claimin' her."

"Oh, really? Why'd you put her in your room then?" Of course Havoc would have noticed that.

"Where the fuck else was I supposed to put her? Ain't like this is a fuckin' hotel."

"Coulda left her in Mercedes's room. Bitch ain't likely to come back anytime soon."

"It's the 'likely' part that had me concerned. You honestly want a cat fight on your hands?" When Thorn grinned, Vicious heaved a sigh. "I mean minus the Jell-O or pudding."

Finally, Thorn chuckled, Havoc joining in. "Fine, Vicious. Deny it all you want, but I think you're staking a claim. Maybe for the short term, but you don't put her in your room otherwise. You give her to one of the club girls, and they deal with her. Now, you're stuck with a woman *and* jealous club girls. Honestly, how do you manage to get such a fuckin' followin'?"

Vicious cupped his crotch. "Gotta have the right equipment and know how to use it, bro. Club girls love a man with skill *and* beef."

Havoc howled his laughter. "He got you there, prez."

Thorn wasn't put out at all. In fact, he looked satisfied. Probably could sense how restless Vicious was getting talking about the girl waiting in his room. Thorn knew his men better than they knew themselves sometimes.

"Let me know if anything develops. Also, I want eyes on El Diablo and Black Reign. If they so much as take a shit somewhere they don't normally shit, I wanna know about it."

"I'll get Ripper on it. If he needs equipment we don't have, I'll get him to borrow it from Data. Might take a few days to get everything set up."

"Not a problem. Until then, I want two men on the Black Reign clubhouse and two on El Diablo around the clock."

Chapter Three

Lucy woke with a blanket tucked securely around her in a warm embrace. The pizza had been *delicious*. In fact, she'd eaten all but one slice. He'd sent beer, too. A six pack. She'd polished off three before she'd finally passed out. Not literally. It had been forever since she'd gotten more than a couple hours' sleep at a time. With a full belly and the alcohol, she'd been so sleepy, all she could do was stumble to the bathroom then lie on the couch. The bed had beckoned, but she wasn't touching it. No fucking way.

As she rubbed her eyes and stretched, she realized she was in the very place she'd avoided. Not only that, she was surrounded by strong arms with her ear resting over the steady drum of a beating heart. A warm, masculine scent surrounded her. Strangely, she wasn't scared. She should be, but it just wasn't there.

"Have a good sleep?" God, could that voice be any sexier? She recognized Vicious, but now he sounded more erotic than scary.

"How long have I been out?" She tried to move off him, but his arms were unbreakable bands around her. If she were honest, it felt too nice to struggle much.

"Oh, about twelve hours. I found you on the couch, shivering. Don't expect that to happen again."

"Falling asleep on the couch without a blanket?"

"Fallin' asleep on the couch, period. You want to sleep, you crawl into the bed and cover up. You'll be warm and comfortable."

"Believe me, the couch was comfortable."

"Not like the bed." One hand began to stroke soothingly over her through the blanket. Never into forbidden territory, but he showed no signs of stopping. His hands were so big he spanned her whole back. Lucy remembered how big he was and could only imagine how she looked lying there against his chest. Probably like a child.

"Are you always so bossy?"

He chuckled. "Oh, baby girl, you have no idea." She sighed, then pushed off him, intending to get up. Again, he held her fast. "Where you goin'?"

"Well, as you pointed out, I've been asleep for twelve hours. I had three beers before going to sleep. The bathroom would be my very best friend right now."

For several moments he didn't move. Then he let out a resigned sigh. "Fine. But I want you back here the second you're done. We need to talk."

Several questions went through her mind, but Lucy wasn't voicing any of them yet. She scrambled off the bed and into the bathroom, locking the door behind her. Strangely, she felt cold and... unhappy now that she was away from him.

Vicious...

Yeah. If ever there was a man she needed to avoid, it was this one. He could break her in half if he chose. And what did she really know about this group? Black Reign wasn't cruel to her, or, at least, not that she'd witnessed. The women had never spoken about being mistreated or made to do anything they hadn't wanted to do. Even though she'd been asked to dance for parties and privately for Rycks, no one had made unwanted advances on her, and no one had suggested she do anything other than dance. They paid her well for that service, not counting tips. Better than she'd ever made at the club, even with tips and lap dances.

Then Rycks had sent her here. Obviously, he hadn't given this club the heads-up she was coming. Her first instinct to hide her presence had been the best idea. So how did she deal with Vicious? If he was planning to hurt her, she doubted he'd have let her have a good night's sleep beforehand. It probably wasn't the smartest decision she'd ever make, but she was going to take things at face value. If he proved he intended her harm, she'd backtrack and regroup.

As she washed her hands, Lucy looked into the mirror at herself. Without makeup or her hair styled, she looked like a lost waif. A far cry from the exotic dancer she transformed herself into. Her hair was in a messy bun out of her way for sleep, little curls slipping free.

She brushed a stray curl out of her face before heaving a little sigh. Which was when she noticed a toothbrush in the package lying on the vanity. With a shrug, she opened it and used it. It was amazing how much better she felt after brushing her teeth. So, she decided to wash her face as well. Her clothes weren't the freshest, but she felt a hundred percent better.

When she exited the bathroom, she found Vicious still stretched out on the bed, his hands behind his head. He looked like he was dozing, but she had the feeling he was all too aware of her. A quick glance at the windows let her know it was dark outside. If she'd slept for twelve hours, it was probably three or four in the morning.

"Come on," he said, not opening his eyes. "Back up here with ya."

"If we're going to talk, shouldn't we sit somewhere?"

"No. We're doin' it just like we were when you woke up."

"Why?"

"'Cause I said so, girl. Now get up here before I take you over my knee."

OK, *that* brought her up short. "Excuse me?"

"You heard me. There are rules here. You follow them or you get punished." He still didn't open his eyes, and Lucy was certain she saw a faint smile on his face, but in the dim lighting, she couldn't be sure.

"I never heard any of the other girls talk about getting hit. I think that would have been something I'd have heard about."

"No one said anything about being hit. But being *spanked* is a completely different experience."

Unbidden, the image of her lying across Vicious's lap while he spanked her bare bottom flashed through her head, and she nearly whimpered. Why in the world was that image so hot? That totally wasn't her scene. In fact, she avoided any form of pain for any reason. His warm chuckle said he was, indeed, paying very close attention to her.

With a huff, she threw herself onto the bed, crossing her arms over her chest as she lay on the opposite side from him. No way she was going to get into an argument with him over something like that when the very idea turned her on so fast, she had no hope of controlling her reaction.

She figured Vicious would demand she drape herself over him like she had been, but instead he chuckled before rolling over and blanketing himself over her. One heavy thigh pinned hers, and one obscenely muscled arm wound around her upper body. His face rested against her hair as he snuggled against her, settling them both under the blanket, their heads sharing one pillow.

"Uh, what the hell do you think you're doing?"

"Getting comfortable."

"I feel compelled to point out we'd be just as comfortable *sitting* on the couch."

"I disagree." His voice rumbled through her body, so she had to stifle a shiver. Why in the world she was attracted to this type of man she had no idea. Hell, the whole time she was in the Black Reign clubhouse she hadn't been attracted to the men there. Sure, some of them had been sexy and even charming, but it was all part of the job to her. Maybe that was the problem. This wasn't a job. But what if she could make it one?

"Fine. Talk. Then I can get a shower and start the day."

"It's three in the morning. Anyone up this hour ain't gonna want you to be startin' your day. They're gonna be wantin' services I'm not sure you'd want to provide."

"Is that what this is about?" She tried to look at him, but he simply nuzzled her head until she turned back and he settled against her once again. "You think I intend to earn my keep on my back?"

He shrugged. "On your back. On your knees. Whatever." She was about to give him what for when he laughed. "I can see gettin' your back up is gonna be the highlight of my day."

"You're a swine!"

"Relax, Lucy. You're safe here. But we've got to set up an arrangement between the two of us. You're not ready to be turned loose in the club, and you don't have the disposition of a club girl."

"Oh, really? I did just fine in Black Reign."

"How'd you earn your keep?"

Jesus. Did she really want to do this again? Rycks hadn't taken advantage of her. Would Vicious?

"That's none of your business."

"I only ask because everyone earns their keep here. If you're here as a club girl or patch chaser you'll be expected to service the men who want it."

"I just knew you'd say that," she bit out. It wasn't unexpected, but she couldn't deny she was disappointed. "Let me up."

"You just stay right here, baby girl."

"I'm not having sex to earn my keep. That's not even on the table. I'd rather leave." Again, she pushed away, kicking out when he wouldn't let her up. "Let me go, you asshole!"

"Calm the fuck down, woman."

"I said, let me go!"

"Christ! Would you stop squirming!" Vicious shifted so that he covered her more fully, rolling his hips so that she had to spread her legs.

Lucy couldn't catch her breath. How could she have misjudged this man so badly? "Don't! I didn't agree to this!"

"Calm your tits, woman. I'm not doing anything other than trying to get you to lay still. I'm not gonna hurt you."

"I'm not a whore," she whimpered. "I'm a dancer. That's it!"

He pulled back slightly, giving her a baffled look. "A... dancer?"

"Yes. That's all. I danced for Black Reign. I didn't sleep with any of them."

Vicious took some of his weight from her, but didn't move off. "I ain't makin' you a whore, baby girl. But we need to come to an arrangement to keep you off limits to the other men in Salvation's Bane. Otherwise, you'll have men crawlin' up your ass. So to speak."

Lucy tried to slow her breathing down. She'd never been so frightened. Probably because she had no idea where she stood with Vicious. He could do whatever he wanted, yet he didn't seem to be progressing the situation any further. She closed her eyes and took several deep breaths, finding her focus. It was similar to the way she felt before a performance. All she had to do was get a hold of herself.

* * *

There was a moment when Vicious could see Lucy panic. Her eyes were wide and wild, their golden color almost completely consumed by the dark pupil. She had been afraid he was going to force himself on her, yet she worked her way through it. He could see it in her eyes. And he was a bastard for pushing her. No man should have done that and not gotten castrated, yet there he was. He'd tried to sooth her fears, but he hadn't moved off her. He wanted her to accept that he wouldn't harm her, to come to the conclusion on her own and accept his dominance.

Because he was a bastard.

She looked up with those lovely, lovely eyes of hers. Sweet. Innocent. She was slight of form, so much smaller than him. So delicate. He stroked her shiny hair, her cheekbones. The petal-soft skin of her lips beckoned him, but he didn't dare kiss her. Not yet. Not now. She'd lose her mind.

She closed her eyes briefly, taking several breaths. Calming herself. When she opened her eyes again, she met his boldly. No fear shown there, or resignation. Only a trust he didn't deserve, and she shouldn't give.

"What do you want from me?" Though her voice shook, she held his gaze boldly. A brave little warrior.

"I want you to stay here with me. You'll be my woman for all intents and purposes. You'll stay in my room. Wear my property patch. I won't touch you other than to sleep with you at night unless we're in public, but only to keep appearances."

"Why? Why not just say I'm off limits?"

He raised an eyebrow. "Did Rycks do that?"

"Well, no. But he didn't claim either me or Mae either. His brothers just knew."

"He didn't claim you conventionally. But I'm willing to bet he warned off every single man in that club." What Vicious held back from her was that no one in his club would ever touch her unless she invited it whether she was claimed or not. He was just being a bastard and wanting to make sure no one touched her even if she did invite it.

She shrugged. "Maybe. I got hit on, but not seriously. Mae didn't at all."

"I could probably work out something like that, but I'm not taking any chances. You're not here for any reason other than to wait for your sister."

"I can dance, you know. It worked with Black Reign. I danced three or four nights a week in the common room. It was pretty much just like working a club except the pay was better. Anyone hitting on me took 'no' for an answer and tipped extra. I don't mind doing that here to earn my keep."

Something inside Vicious threatened to burst out of him. It was ugly and mean. Possessive to a fault. No way he wanted other men to see her naked body. "That pleasure is only for me, baby girl. You wanna dance for me? I'll definitely take it. But no one else. Not here."

"Then I guess we have a deal. I'm here until Rycks and El Diablo find my sister. I'm comfortable with dancing."

"Bane is looking for your sister, too. I dare say we'll find her before Black Reign does. Assuming they're even looking for her."

"Believe me. Rycks is looking for Mae. I think he sees himself as her protector."

"Any chance he arranged for her to be taken? You know. Like away from the club so he could have her for himself?"

Lucy shook her head. "It wasn't like that. Besides, he already kept her away from the clubhouse as much as possible. Both of us. I was there at night, but he took me back to the estate he and El Diablo and El Segador shared."

"I take it the three of them were close." Vicious didn't like where this was going.

"Yes. I think they'd been together long before any of them came to Black Reign. Rycks was there first but he is solidly El Diablo's man."

"And this El Segador?"

She shivered, looking away from Vicious for the first time. "He's not like any person I've ever met. If I didn't know better, I'd swear he didn't have a soul." As she talked to him, Lucy relaxed under his hold. A good sign. "He's the man who makes their problems go away. From what I saw, if he went after someone, his solutions were permanent, if you know what I mean."

"I get you. Did he ever harm you or threaten you in anyway?"

"Never. But I didn't interact with him at all. As far as I know, neither did Mae. Rycks kept us as far away from El Segador as he could."

All this was more than Vicious could wrap his head around at the moment. He hadn't had enough rest, what with the meetings with Thorn and Havoc and the members of Bones actively working on the problem. He'd only been in bed a couple hours when Lucy had roused. Now, he just wanted a couple more hours.

"We'll talk more later." He rolled over to his side, taking her with him and positioning her so she was spooned against him. "Right now, I need a fuckin' nap."

She was silent. Vicious had nearly drifted off when she spoke again. "You know, I could sleep on the couch."

"Already discussed that. Ain't as comfortable as the bed."

"Then you sleep on the couch."

He grunted, repeating, "Ain't as comfortable as the bed."

"You're an ass, you know that?"

Vicious couldn't help the grin tugging at his lips. "Maybe. But I'm going to be a comfortable ass."

She giggled, and everything in Vicious settled. He couldn't do the things to her little body he wanted to -- yet -- but she would be his as much as he could manage.

Lucy settled against him, snuggling into his embrace. It wasn't long before her breathing was deep and even, letting Vicious know she'd dozed off. Though he was bone tired, he found it hard to actually sleep. There was too much on his mind. Mostly, what to do about this whole situation.

One thing at a time. They had to find Mae. Once they did, they'd work out a rescue plan, most likely with Black Reign, though he didn't trust those motherfuckers any farther than he could spit. With the other club or without them, Vicious knew Thorn would have contacted Black Reign so the two clubs didn't up killing each other in the crossfire.

Though he didn't think he'd be able to go to sleep, no matter how tired he was, Lucy's warm body pressed tightly against him, the trusting way she slept so peacefully in his arms, relaxed him more than anything had in memory. With a final sigh, Vicious closed his eyes and slept.

Chapter Four

"You've got a lot of fuckin' explainin' to do, El Diablo." Thorn let his voice mirror his anger. It took more than a minor nuisance to get Thorn's back up, but this whole situation was more than disrespectful. It could potentially put the club at risk. Vicious was sure it had been a very long time since he'd seen his president this angry. "Sendin' that girl here had less to do with keepin' her safe and more to do with seein' how far you could fuckin' push me, you bastard."

There was a pause in Thorn's tirade as El Diablo spoke on the other end of the phone before Thorn continued. "I could give a good Goddamn! My only concern is keepin' my club safe and off the radar. You've practically shoved us under the microscope!" Another pause. "You listen to me, you son of a bitch. The only reason I'm not goin' to war with you is because one of my men is claimin' the girl. She wants her sister back, so we'll do that. But, understand me, anyone -- and I mean anyone -- comes after Mae once we have her, I will bring hellfire and the Holy Ghost down on you so hard you'll wish your friends had gotten ahold of you first." With that, Thorn ended the call.

"Sounded like that went well," Havoc drawled. "Thought we weren't gettin' involved?"

"Fuckin' bastard forced my hand." Thorn looked at Torpedo. "Any word from Data?" It had been several days since they started their hunt. Their brothers in Bones MC in Kentucky had come in handy with their resources. Vicious was also glad he'd had this time to gain Lucy's trust. He still had a long way to go, but he'd coaxed a few smiles and even a little laughter from her. The sound was so magical he found he was living for that fucking sound. It was pathetic, and if his brothers ever found out he'd never hear the end of it.

"Expecting something any time now. They're tryin' to confirm, but, once he brought Azriel in from Shadow Demons, they think they know who's got Mae, and why they're after El Diablo."

Thorn raised an eyebrow. "Oh?"

Vicious shrugged. "That's what he says. Won't speculate, though. Says he needs to be sure before accusing anyone. Apparently, this is some serious shit El Diablo's into."

"He's a killer for hire! How much more serious can it get?"

"Pretty serious. Data says even Azriel is upset about this one. Some kind of untouchable group or somethin'. He won't say more than that."

"He say how much longer he needed?"

"Couple of days?"

"How much time do we have before they start sending Mae back in pieces? I mean, do we have any idea where they're holding her? 'Cause I'm sure your woman wants her back whole."

"None. Whoever took her got away clean. Even Data can't find exactly where and when they took her. These guys are good."

Thorn's gaze hardened. "We've got to be better. Havoc, make sure everything is ready to roll once we know where to go. When we find these fucks, I want to send a message."

"Anything in particular?" Havoc leaned against the wall, idly cleaning under his nails with a knife.

"Yeah. I want them to understand they don't strike out at women and children to get at their enemies. If they've harmed Mae in any way, I want every single last mother fucker dead."

A satisfied calm fell over Vicious. This was one order he could and would follow to the letter.

After their meeting was over, Vicious headed back to his room. He'd left Lucy there by herself. She'd been pretty much locked in there for the better part of a week. Not only was she beginning to feel pinned in, she was growing ever anxious about her sister. Fortunately, he had proof-of-life photos for her El Diablo had sent. Data had done some super-secret computer-geek stuff and determined they were legitimate and not some fabricated images designed to mislead them. As of twelve hours earlier, Mae was alive and well. They'd taken pictures of her riding a horse. She'd been all smiles and seemed oblivious to the fact she was in danger. They had no idea who she was with or where she was, but Data and Azriel were both doing everything they could to figure it out. Unless something had changed after that photo -- which was entirely possible -- at least the girl seemed oblivious to the danger she was in. Hopefully, that would ease Lucy's mind until they had a working plan.

With that in mind, Vicious headed back to his room. The music hit him long before he reached his door. It was a strange mix of hip-hop and funk or soul. A slow, sensual number but not a normal ballad. This music was specifically crafted for seduction. Carefully, he opened the door…

And nearly fell to his knees.

In the middle of the room, Lucrecia… danced. Her hips snapped occasionally side to side or front to back with the beat of the music. Other times, she swayed, turning her body around and around, giving glimpses of her luscious curves. She was dressed in a tight-fitting tank and boy shorts. Not underwear, but tight fitting, as if she didn't want them getting in her way and needed the freedom of movement.

She was oblivious to his presence, which Vicious was grateful for. He had a feeling that, if she knew he was watching her, she'd stop. Nothing in this world could make him announce his presence if it meant she stopped moving. There was a grace to her eroticism, one that spoke of training in more than exotic dancing. This woman knew what she was about. Which begged the question, why was she practicing?

Vicious shut the door softly, not wanting to give away his presence. She continued to move, her body a lesson in erotic movement. Every turn of her wrist, every snap of her hips seemed designed to drive a man fuckin' wild.

She stumbled slightly and Vicious thought she'd probably noticed him in the room. The stumble wasn't overt, but just that little pause in the fluidity of her movements. Swearing softly, she stopped before repeating the movement several times. Then she repeated it again, this time adding a few steps before and after it. Once completed, she did it again, this time continuing. If this was her stripper routine -- and, really, what else could she use it for? -- it was far more than he'd ever suspected went into something like an exotic dance. She was obviously so engrossed she wasn't paying attention to anything around her, even the fact that she was no longer alone.

The dance continued as if nothing had been amiss. So lovely. Lustful. A dance so seductive it was all Vicious could do not to go to her.

Lucy. *His* Lucy. She was more than any woman he'd ever known. So beautiful. Innocent, yet passionate. No woman could dance like that and not need a man as desperately as she made him need her. Her every movement, though understated, seemed calculated to entice a man to madness. Vicious was sure that, if he watched her for long, he'd give her anything she wanted if she'd just let him have her.

Absently, Vicious sat in a chair situated in the corner next to the window. He watched as her dance increased in speed. It was as if the more aroused she became, the faster she moved. Her expression was one of ecstasy, her eyes half closed as she moved around the room. So graceful and beautiful. Nothing he'd ever witnessed was as beautiful as this woman in this moment.

He did his best not to make a sound, but the moment she started shedding clothing, he knew he was in trouble. She wasn't obvious about it. One second, she wore a garment, the next it fluttered to the floor at her feet. The woman had the most beautiful breasts he'd ever seen. Perfectly formed and topped with dusky pink nipples, they called to him. Beckoned him to touch. Taste. Her torso rippled with fine muscle, as if she'd been honed by the dancing she did. Twirling around several times, she let her bottoms fall to her ankles. With one deft kick, they landed in the corner next to the bathroom. The move was effortless, as though she'd done it countless times and perfected not only the placement of garment, but the ease with which she put it there.

Once completely nude, she raised her arms over her head and moved in a circle, her hips leading the movement with little twists and snaps. Her body undulated in abandon. A little smile graced her face along with a look something like euphoria. Unless Vicious was mistaken, Lucy got a kind of high from dancing. She didn't even need an audience. Just the music.

And her very nude body.

She continued to dance, completely oblivious to the fact she wasn't alone in the room. Vicious continued to watch in rapt fascination, hardly daring to breathe lest he give away his presence and break the spell.

The door to his room opened, and Thorn stepped inside. "Holy shit!"

Immediately, Vicious was on his feet, putting his body between Lucy and Thorn. "What the fuck?" he bit out as softly as he could at his long-time friend. "Knock first, you bastard!" He tried not to draw Lucy's attention, but it was far too late, thanks to Thorn's less-than-subtle entrance. She'd already become aware of them and, worse, let out a distressed cry before heading to the bathroom. "Goddamn it, Thorn," Vicious snarled.

"Hey, sorry, brother." Thorn raised his hands in surrender. "Didn't know you were having a private party."

"Ain't. Now get the fuck out."

"Just wanted to invite the little lady downstairs for the cookout." He raised an eyebrow. "We good?"

"Depends. You gonna make a play for her?"

Thorn grinned. "Not likely. I'm a mean, tough son of a bitch, but I'm not suicidal."

Vicious nodded satisfied. Then stopped. "Wait. What exactly does that mean?"

"It means, brother, I ain't fightin' you over a woman. Especially not one you're so far gone over."

"What the fuck'er you talkin' about? I'm not gone. I just don't want anyone taking advantage. She's not like the women here."

"Oh, believe me. I'm fully aware. If any of our club girls could move like that, we'd be havin' parties all the Goddamned time. That girl's got talent."

"Get the fuck out." Vicious wanted to pound his friend, but it would only play into Thorn's hands. The chuckle from Thorn said the man was, indeed, trying to make him snap just to prove his point. Vicious could deny it to himself and Lucy all he wanted, but in his mind, Vicious had already claimed the tiny little dancer currently hiding out in his bathroom.

Well, fuck.

* * *

Oh, God. *Oh, God!* She was so fucked. There was no way she could fight either of them off and definitely not both of them together. She'd locked the door, but there was no doubt in her mind either of them could break in and drag her out. Thank God she'd intended to shower later and left a T-shirt and underwear in the bathroom.

There was a soft knock at the door. "Lucy. It's OK. Open the door."

"I'm not coming out there," she said, her voice wobbling.

"Yes. You are. Now, please. Open up."

"I shouldn't have been practicing." That part was her fault. "If I gave you the wrong impression, I'm sorry. I don't do anything but dance."

"Woman, has anyone made a move on you?"

She opened her mouth but closed it almost immediately. "Well, no."

"Then give me the benefit of the doubt, girl."

"You slept with me."

"Yeah. And did we do anything other than sleep? Did I touch you inappropriately?"

Why did he have to be so reasonable? She had a right to be upset! With that calm, soothing tone he used, she found her anxiety melting away. Yeah. Vicious might have a scary name, but the man wasn't a bad guy. At least, not to her.

Lucy opened the door a crack to see Vicious looking down at her. She was surprised to see a concerned look on his face. Like he didn't like that she'd been distressed.

"You OK? I'm not gonna let anyone here hurt you." He shook his head as if what he said wasn't exactly what he intended to say. "Ain't lettin' no one *anywhere* hurt you." Lucy thought it was telling that he qualified the statement before she'd even mentioned it.

"It's fine. I shouldn't have been practicing like that. Especially not a full, er, *un*dress rehearsal." She tried to use humor to defuse the situation. "I just… it's soothing." She looked at her feet. "Sometimes."

He pushed the door open the rest of the way and held out his hand for her. "Come back in here. We'll talk."

"What if I don't want to talk?"

His lips quirked as if he found her amusing. "We'll talk anyway. Come on."

With a sigh, Lucy took his hand. It swallowed her smaller one like an adult taking a child's hand. Given her interaction with him before when he'd insisted on talking with her in the bed, in his arms, she fully expected him to insist they do the same now. But he didn't. There was no reason to, and he obviously wasn't trying to make her uncomfortable. Instead, he led her to the couch before taking a chair across from her.

"Look at me, Lucy." She thought about being stubborn, but she knew she'd never win a battle of wills with him. When she raised her head, she met those harsh, dark eyes of his. Who wouldn't be intimidated by this man? He was big, scary, and so very intense. When he looked at her, Lucy got the impression he could see straight through her soul. "No one is going to make you do anything you don't want to do. You walk out into the common room naked or dancing like you were, I guarantee you'll get cat calls, and whistles, and probably get hit on, but no one is going to touch you if you don't want to be touched. And no one will ridicule you for teasing them. More likely, they'll throw money at you to keep it up just so they can see that lovely little body of yours."

OK, that *really* shouldn't have sounded as good as it did. Not that she wanted strange men looking at her -- she'd never really thought about it after the first couple times she'd danced. Oh, no. She found she loved the fact that he thought she had a lovely body. *Him*. Vicious. No one else.

He cleared his throat. "So, if you need to dance, you can do it for me. I'll make sure no one can interrupt us, and you'll know no one will be able to get past me to get to you. Sound reasonable?"

Yes. Totally. "Are you kidding me? No, it's not reasonable!"

"You need to dance? That's the only way it's happenin'." His face was hard, and Lucy knew he meant business.

"Then I won't do it at all." She was being stubborn, but there was no way in hell she was going to agree to this. Not now. She'd been there before, and it hadn't been that bad, but there was no way lightning could strike twice. There were only so many times one could bait a tiger.

"Yes. You will. In fact, I insist on it."

"Is this a condition of my sanctuary?"

"Nope." He grinned at her. "Just gratitude on your part for me allowing you the comfort of my room instead of putting you in a smaller one in the middle of all the club girls."

"I'll be perfectly fine in a room of my own! Why would you think I wouldn't be?"

"Never said it was for your benefit. It's a luxury for you. Not something you need or even want, but a definite upgrade."

"Oh? Well, the price is too steep --"

"It's for my benefit you stay here. And you're going to dance for me, because I happen to think you enjoy it just enough to wonder what my reaction would be if you gave me a full performance."

She started to say something then shut her mouth. Finally, she shook her head. "You've lost your mind."

"Have I?" He raised an eyebrow at her. "Then why are you blushing so becomingly? I think you want to dance for me. You like the idea that you can trust me not to take advantage of the situation, but are just scared enough to wonder if I'm lying." His grin was positively wicked. "And I think it turns you on."

"OK. That's it. I'm leaving now."

"You could," he said, still not letting go of her hand. In fact, he rubbed it lightly, his big, rough hands playing gently over her delicate skin. "Or you could live on the wild side. Think of it. You'll have a rapt audience every single night."

"And you'll just let me go to bed alone."

"Oh, hell no," he responded instantly. "I already told you. Couch ain't as comfortable as the bed, and I'm gonna be comfortable. So are you. We'll sleep together in that big bed. You might even feel my hard cock nestling between the cheeks of your ass when I pull your body against mine, but you're going to sleep in that bed with me. I'm going to torture myself because I like knowing you're within arm's reach. And, when you wake up in the morning, we'll go about our business in front of the club. No one will know we're *not* having sex and, therefore, no one will hit on you whether you flirt with them or not."

"I still don't understand why we have to sleep in the same bed."

"Did you hear Thorn knock before entering my room?"

She blinked. "Well, no. But I wasn't exactly paying attention."

"Sweetheart, you didn't hear him because he didn't fuckin' knock. And the doors ain't got locks on 'em."

"Oh. So, if someone came in before we got up, it wouldn't do for them to see one of us sleeping on the couch."

He smiled broadly. "Now you've got it."

She sighed. "You're so full of shit. That's the biggest ruse ever to get me to sleep with you, but I'm going to go out on a limb. Mainly because it was kind of nice before."

"Good. Now that that's settled, finish gettin' dressed and we'll go grab a bite to eat. Apparently, they're havin' a small party downstairs, which always means good food, and I'm starvin'."

The party was in full swing when they arrived. Lucy was surprised at how tame it was. Sure there were women hanging on to the men, but everyone was dressed and halfway sober. For now. The parties she'd been to with Black Reign had been much less subdued.

Well, the night was young. It would probably get going soon enough.

Vicious led her to a long table where a huge spread of burgers, hotdogs, and all the trimmings was laid out. A big man with a booming laugh and a vest labeled "Red" on the back manned the grill. He caught sight of them and waved them over.

"Whatcha got there, brother? Nice little bit of beautiful." Red eyed Lucy up and down. It seemed more curious than insulting, but Vicious shoved her farther behind him. Just a little.

"Her name's Lucrecia. Goes by Lucy, and she's *very* off limits."

A huge smile split Red's face. "Off limits means only until I charm her away from you." He turned his attention to Lucy and winked. "Welcome, little miss. Don't give it to this guy. Any babies he makes would look like him, and no one wants that."

Lucy was surprised to find herself grinning. "Good to know someone's watching out for me. Thanks for the tip."

Vicious scowled and snagged her hand. "Come on. Let's find Thorn and introduce you properly."

"Wait. Thorn? The guy who walked in on me?"

"Yeah. Don't worry. He won't bite too hard."

"Do we have to?" It was adorable the way she bit her lower lip, but he didn't want her distressed.

"Yes. You're a guest in his house. Man rightly likes to know who's sleeping under his roof."

"Why do you have to be so fucking reasonable?" She muttered her question but followed him without him having to force her.

Thorn was standing with a group of other Salvation's Bane members. He had one foot on the bench of a picnic table, beer in hand. They were laughing at something one of the prospects had said when Vicious approached them.

"Thorn." He greeted the other man with a firm handshake.

"Glad you could join us, brother. I see you brought the young lady with you." Thorn turned his cold blue eyes Lucy's way. She had to force herself not to shift behind Vicious. Like he'd be any help. He was the one who'd brought her to the man in the first place. She was surprised when a low, rumbling growl came from Vicious. Thorn raised an eyebrow and glanced his way but said nothing.

Vicious cleared his throat. "This is Lucrecia. I'd like her to stay here until we locate her sister." If that was Vicious's idea of asking, it was likely to get her thrown out on her ear. But then, MCs seemed to have a different set of social rules.

"Lucrecia." Thorn extended a hand to her. "You're welcome, of course. Make sure Vicious explains the rules to you, follow them, and you should be fine."

"I -- rules?" She sounded like a little mouse and hated it. One thing she'd learned during her time with Black Reign was that she had to be strong to survive. This first meeting would set the tone for her entire stay.

"Gotta have 'em."

She squared her shoulders and met his gaze boldly. "Every place does. I can earn my keep and do my part of the chores. I don't expect a free ride."

Thorn raised his eyebrows and glanced sharply at Vicious. "We can always use another hand with the cooking and cleaning." When Vicious took a step forward, pushing her behind him slightly, Lucy stiffened and moved away from him.

"Look, I'm not going to be a club whore. But I'm a damned good cook, and my cleaning skills are better than what you've obviously got going on currently." She made her expression as hard as she could. "This place was a pig sty a couple of weeks ago."

With a soft chuckle Thorn raised his beer in salute to her. "I take it that was you cleaning up after us. Girls were trying to take the credit, but we all knew better. They're all a little spoiled."

"Believe me. I noticed. They'd've been kicked out at Black Reign. That club doesn't tolerate the club girls not pulling their weight." She was trying to be hard, but she was terribly afraid, despite Vicious's assurance, they'd still want her to dance. Though she loved dancing, she really didn't want the same setup she had with Black Reign. It was bad enough Vicious wanted her to do it for him.

OK. That wasn't entirely accurate. She was good with dancing for Vicious. Suspected she was more than good with it. Could she actually be looking forward to it?

Fuck.

Thorn chuckled. "Yeah. This is gonna be interesting."

"Thorn." Vicious found her hand and she let him. "We already talked about this."

"I'm well aware." He brought his gaze back to Lucy. "We'll try you cooking. Your responsibility will be the kitchen. You need help, you tell Vicious and he gets you help. Otherwise, the other girls will be responsible for the rest of the clubhouse. If it turns out you can't cook to our liking, we'll shift duties around. And, little girl..." Thorn took a step toward her, his expression amused as he leaned down to put his face in front of hers. "No one here whores unless they want to. Some girls like the excitement and the money. Others prefer to stick to one man at a time. Get me?" He waited until she nodded her understanding. "Good. Now." He waved his hand at the party that was now well underway around them. "Get to know everyone. Have a good time. We don't usually do breakfast, but people start wandering to the kitchen for lunch around eleven. That work for you?"

All she could do was nod. Did he intimidate her? Hell, yes, he did. All of a sudden, she realized how tightly she was gripping Vicious's hand and realized that, on some level, she trusted the big man.

Well, shit.

Chapter Five

As club parties went, this turned out to be about the norm. The music was a touch different, but Lucy could deal. Seemed like a few of their club girls decided a healthy dose of industrial metal or something close was in the works. Five Finger Death Punch, God Module, Megaherz, and Rammstein blasted loud enough it was hard to talk over top of it. Which was fine with her. She was observing. It was how she'd survive in this new place.

So far, she was seeing the usual hierarchy of MC society. The men all deferred to Thorn, the president, and the women seemed to be ranked either by how long they'd been with the club or the bed of the man they were currently sharing. None of these men had ol' ladies so no one woman could claim dominance over everyone else. There were a few who tried, but it was a struggle. And yes, the women seemed to actually be more aggressive than the men. Which was awesome.

Not.

The men seemed to indulge the women more than Black Reign ever did, but they were still the dominants and had the last say in the event of an argument. Lucy thought there might be a problem with the music selection, but the local favorite, God Module, won everyone over. Thorn, however, made it clear that if the women wanted to keep their music, they had to make it worth their while. Naturally, the clothes came off soon after.

While most of the women welcomed Lucy, if a bit coolly, the ones vying for dominance were standoffish. Not that she cared. She was here until Salvation's Bane found her sister, then she was gone, something she made very clear to the women. Last thing she wanted was for them to think she was trying to put her nose in their pack. Once word got around, more women approached her, all bearing liquor of some kind. Beer, but mostly whisky. Just great.

"I don't suppose you'd understand if I told you anything harder than beer didn't agree with me, would you?"

The blonde bombshell dressed in leather pants and a leather tank that pushed her boobs nearly to her chin laughed. It was obvious this was Lucy's first test. "Nonsense! You're a big girl." She looked Lucy up and down with a superior air. "Drink up... Lucy." The women with her tittered, as if Lucy's name was the height of hilarity. This was the part she hated. She didn't like having to prove her worth or her fortitude. She just wanted to... *be*.

With a sigh, she accepted the shot from the blonde -- Claws, apparently because she had two-inch-long pointed nails that looked sharp as daggers. Definitely not a woman Lucy wanted to get in a scuffle with. Meeting the woman's eye as she braced herself for the burn of the whisky, Lucy downed it. Thankfully, she was able to keep her face carefully blank. The women laughed, a couple scowling as they handed money over. Obviously there had been bets placed.

"Good. Join the party. It'll move to the beach soon. Bonfire is almost ready."

Great. A bonfire with a bunch of bikers. What could go wrong?

While the clubhouse was in a relatively urban area, there was enough space around them for the party not to bother neighbors too much. The beach was adjacent to the property and looked to have been sectioned off, letting visitors know they weren't welcome. Right.

By the time she'd finished her third beer and fifth shot of whisky, Lucy knew she was done. If she did more, she'd lose any sense she had.

"You good?" The rumbly voice next to her ear wouldn't have nearly such a sexual effect on her had she not been two-thirds drunk. She was positive.

"Never better." She smiled brightly over her shoulder at him.

God, the man was devastating. That dark beard and the tattoo creeping up his neck gave him just enough bad-boy appearance to remind her of what he was, but, also, just enough bad-boy appearance to make her wet.

"You too drunk to go to the beach?" His grin was at once sexy and infuriating, his hands settling on her hips. Normally, she'd have rebuffed him, but she really liked his hands on her. Wanted more of it.

"You asking the other girls that same question?" Lucy did her best to look stern. "'Cause if you're not, you best not treat me any differently."

He raised his eyebrows. "Oh, *now* you don't want to be treated different? Wasn't that long ago you were telling Thorn what you would and wouldn't do. Don't remember any of the other club girls doin' that."

"Ain't a club girl," she said, uncomfortably aware her words were slurring slightly. Maybe he didn't notice. "I won't be here that long so I was just making it clear that I will not be a club whore."

"Look, I'm not your babysitter. I just see the way you're interacting with everyone, having a good time, and I don't want you to get in over your head. It's because I know you don't want to fuck anyone to earn your keep that I'm asking. You go to the bonfire, you'll get caught up in this like everyone else. I guarantee, you'll end up on your back. The girls here have all set their boundaries with the men. You ain't."

"You telling me they'd take advantage of a drunk woman?"

He winced slightly, but shook his head. "Not intentionally. The women here get drunk on purpose." He shrugged. "Claim it makes aggressive sex more fun and relaxes them for anal sex."

Lucy jumped out of his grasp, backing away from him. No way she could prevent the blush creeping up her neck. The big grin on his face said he'd gotten exactly the reaction from her he wanted. "Motherfucker," she grumbled. His booming laughter followed her as she joined a group of women headed to the beach.

* * *

Was goading a woman ever so much fun? He just knew he'd get her back up with that drunk comment, but couldn't help himself. He was paying for it now. Kind of. She was off, having a good time with the club girls -- currently dumping the liquor down her, probably hoping she'd do something embarrassing -- and she was definitely getting drunk. Well, drunk*er*.

The girls were in a feisty mood, considering the music choice. Hard, screamy, and loud, it was going full blast just like at the clubhouse. The guys mostly sat back and watched the show as the women danced and enticed. It didn't take long for the clothing to fall off, either.

Vicious kept a close eye on Lucy. So far, she'd resisted attempts from the men and women to remove her top, but he could tell it wouldn't be long. All around her, women danced. It was almost as surreal a sight as Vicious had ever seen. She looked like some innocent maiden entering a pagan ritual, like a sacrifice. Or perhaps Alice in the rabbit hole. The breeze off the ocean increased, whipping her hair around her in a frenzy. OK, now *she* looked like a pagan.

The music was pounding, a driving hard metal that just beat into a person. The club girls were all around the bonfire in various stages of undress. Bodies gyrated in violent jerks all around Lucy. She just moved in the flow within the large circle. Her gaze seemed focused on the women around her. She didn't dance so much as just move with them, like she was feeling out the situation, yet in some kind of alcohol-induced trance. With every rotation around the fire, she moved with the music a little more, her body adapting to the harsher rhythms. Before long, she was dancing with abandon, moving with the other women, yet apart.

That Lucy was a born dancer there was no question. Even with all her clothes on, her movements were more... polished? No. That wasn't the right word. The music she'd danced to in his room was a world away from the music now, yet she moved like she'd been made specifically for *this*. If she'd been on a stage with Till Lindermann and the rest of Rammstein, no one would have been able to tell she was the outsider. Even her appearance seemed to change. Before, she'd been this angelic innocent among witches. Now, she was a predator. Eyes glazed as she focused on the fire, she was the most erotic, sensual being he'd ever seen. One with bite. The guitars were a loud buzz in the air, the drums hard and driving into his body. "*Mein Teil*" blasted at full volume. A song about, of all things, cannibalism. If ever there was a man eater, Lucy looked the part.

It also seemed wrong.

Faster and faster she moved, her body more aggressive yet erotic. The men circling the fire had gone still, leaning forward. The women mostly stepped away as she got wilder and wilder. Every so often, if anyone got close to her -- man or woman -- Lucy snarled and snapped at them, never once breaking her dance.

Somehow, her top ended up around her wrist above her head, twirling around her arm with her movements. Bare breasts as pale as silver glimmered in the firelight. With a cry, she let her top go, flinging it into the fire as she moved.

This was wrong. She was drunk and had expressed her desire not to dance for Salvation's Bane like she had Black Reign. Vicious knew she might get caught up in the music, like any dancer might, but if she'd been sober, she would never have done this.

He stood, moving toward the fire. All the club girls had moved out of her way, allowing her the space. Some looked more than disgruntled as she stole their thunder, as well as the attention of the men. Others just seemed in awe of her, lusting after her as much as the men. As Vicious approached, two women spotted him. They moved in his direction, but he waved them off with a flick of his hand. One, Ginger, approached him anyway.

"If it's a wild time you're looking for, you know it's not that little mouse, no matter how bad she dances," Ginger purred, wrapping her arms around Vicious's neck as she pressed her body against him. Knowing what it felt like to have Lucy in his arms, having another woman mashed so intimately against him was uncomfortable. He only wanted one woman this close to him, and she was currently dancing topless like a woman possessed, completely oblivious to the crowd watching her with rapt attention.

"Not now, Ginger," he bit out, taking the woman by the waist and setting her away from him. Without another word or even a glance to see if Ginger took the hint, he continued to intercept Lucy.

As she twirled her way to him, Vicious felt her sex appeal like a punch to the groin. He nearly doubled over, the pain was so intense. Thankfully, the men of Salvation's Bane knew the score. Knew not to touch the little princess currently making a display of herself -- otherwise, he had no doubt she'd be part of an orgy the likes of which had never been seen in these parts. Even now, some of the men had women in their laps either riding them or sucking them off. All while they watched the little erotic goddess dance to the fire gods in blatant offering.

She spun toward him, straight into his arms. Graceful as a cat, she wrapped her arms around his neck, giving him a vacant smile. "Vicious..." His name whispered on her lips was like a coming home. No woman had *ever* had this kind of effect on him. Sweat glistened over her skin like a fine sea mist. Her eyes sparkled in her excitement. Obviously, she was in the midst of an alcohol-enhanced adrenaline rush. She saw him. Recognized him. Gave him a warm, welcoming smile as she pulled herself up to him.

Before he realized she was really doing what he thought she was doing, she pressed her lips against his. Instead of a clumsy, drunken meeting, she kissed him with the same grace with which she danced. Her lips fluttered over his lightly before her tongue swept the seam of his, coaxing his own tongue to dance with hers. For several seconds, Vicious was stunned into submission. Her kisses were so fucking sweet. So arousing he knew if she kept it up he'd take her right there in the sand in front of his brothers and anyone else who happened by. Honor be damned.

Honor.

That one thought brought him up short. Vicious was many things, killer among them, but he would never rape a woman. Lucy wanted him in that moment, he had no doubt. But she wasn't in her right mind, and she'd already told him she wasn't a whore for the club. If he let her do this, let her strip away his control like she was threatening to do, no matter how unintentional, he'd lose any claim to honor he had left. And Lucy would rightly hate him.

With a groan and way more strength than he'd ever thought he possessed, he ended the kiss, pulling her tightly to him so that her breasts were mashed against his chest. "Goddamn," he whispered, looking around him to make sure his brothers had the women firmly in hand. He didn't want any of them near him or Lucy. That would come tomorrow. After she sobered up and felt like it. Looked like her first day at work would have to wait.

He found Thorn's gaze, and the other man grinned and nodded at him. "I'll tell the boys to fend for themselves tomorrow. Look after your wayward girl, there."

Lucy looked up at him just as he shifted her into his arms to carry her back to the clubhouse. "I need you to fuck me, Vicious," she whispered. "So much. Please."

"Shhh, baby. I'll take care of you tonight."

"Swear?"

He groaned. "Every fuckin' day, baby."

Every step back to his room was agony for Vicious. The woman in his arms squirmed, mashing her bare breasts against him. Every time she slid against him he nearly fell to his knees. God, he wanted her! He'd been fighting his attraction since that first meeting, but this was too fucking much. Her slim arms were wrapped around him, and she kissed and sucked at the skin of his neck. Every pull, every lap of her sweet little tongue made his cock throb and ache. How the fuck was he going to get through this with his honor intact?

"Vicious," she purred. "Take me'da bed or lossse me fore'er." She giggled.

"God," he growled. "You're some more temptation, girl. Why the fuck'd you drink so much?" Thank God he recognized the *Top Gun* reference to help him remember how drunk she was.

She giggled again. "Jus' a li'l sas'prilla." He kicked the door to his room shut and gently set her on her feet. Naturally, she swayed slightly, her arm shooting out to grip his shoulder. "Woah."

"Yeah, baby. I know. Here. Let's get you to the bathroom."

Surprisingly, Lucy wasn't as unsteady as he'd feared. After that moment he'd first put her on her feet, she'd regained her equilibrium. As if she just realized she was naked from the waist up, she gasped, covering her breasts with her arms. Watching her come out of the haze around her was heartbreaking.

"Oh, God," she groaned. She braced one hand on the sink and leaned against the vanity. "Oh, God!"

"Relax, sweetheart." Vicious tried his best to soothe her, knowing she was starting to wake up from the adrenaline rush. The alcohol would fade much slower, unfortunately.

"Relax? Oh, God!" Her knees buckled. Thankfully, Vicious was close enough to catch her. "What have I done?"

"Nothing that awful," he murmured. "Nothing no one else didn't do. You just did it better." He tried to grin at her, but was very much afraid it came out a predator's smile.

She looked up at him, a scowl on her lovely, exotic face. "Oh, really? Everyone else stripped and danced around the fire naked?"

"'Course they did. This is a biker club. A biker party. Hell, most everyone who was still there when we left was busy fuckin' where anyone around could see. Much worse'n dancin' topless around the bonfire."

The smile he'd hoped to coax from her didn't happen. Instead, she just ducked her head, one arm still covering her breasts, her slim shoulders shaking.

"Can you get undressed and into the shower? Do you need help?"

"No! I mean, I'm good. Thanks."

Right. "Don't be afraid of me doin' somethin' you don't want. I ain't a good guy by no means, but I swear you're safe with me."

"Really. I'm fine."

She wasn't. He could see that but there was nothing he could do. "I'm leavin' the door partially open. Ain't tryin' to spy on you or anything, just don't want you fallin' or callin' out and me not hearin' you." She glanced back over her shoulder but said nothing. "I'll get you some clothes, then we can go to bed."

"I can't --"

"Just take your shower, baby. Long and hot as you need."

"Aren't drunks supposed to take cold showers?"

"Na. All you get from that is a cold, wet, wide-awake drunk. Best thing to do is to sleep it off. To do that, you need someone watching over you in case you get sick."

"Great," she muttered.

"Take your time. I'll check on you in a few minutes."

* * *

Lucy listened as his footsteps faded before she stepped into the shower and adjusted the temperature. It was no wonder she was in the situation she was in. She knew better than to drink like that, especially when she was in a strange environment. Looking back, she'd known the women were forcing liquor on her. They wanted to see where her boundaries were. Well, they'd definitely found them. Oh, she could have refused, but it would have been just as bad. She'd been fucked either way.

Oh well. It was done. No use crying about it now. She'd just have to hope Vicious could keep the other men off her. Assuming he didn't jump her himself.

No. That wasn't right. If he wanted to jump her, he definitely would have done it when she was busy throwing herself at him. She could still taste the salty spice of his skin where she'd licked and sucked. He'd been nothing but kind to her when she'd *begged* him to fuck her.

"Fuck."

The room still spun slightly so she had to sit on the long bench in the big shower, but at least she could think somewhat clearly. The hot water hitting her body felt like heaven, and it wasn't long before she just laid her head back on the shower wall and closed her eyes.

The next thing she knew, the water was turned off, and someone wrapped a big, fluffy towel around her. She was lifted and set on the vanity top.

"Let's get you dry, girl. Then I'll put you to bed."

"Vicious?" Her eyes were so heavy. The hot shower had definitely done its work. "Please don't hurt me."

"Baby, nothing in the world could make me hurt you, or let anyone else. Rest easy. I'll watch over you."

She let him help dress her then help her climb into bed. He must have put her in one of his shirts because his scent surrounded her, and it was the most comforting thing she'd ever smelled. The last thing she remembered was him settling his body around hers, his strong arms closing around her securely.

* * *

"Fuuuuuck." Lucy groaned as she rolled over. Her mouth tasted like three-day-old shit, and her head was splitting. Her stomach was queasy, but she didn't think she was going to puke just yet. She sat up and carefully swung her legs over the side of the bed. "Fuuuuuck."

"Yeah, baby. Got that the first time."

Her head snapped up to see a grinning Vicious approaching her with a bottle of Gatorade and another of Ibuprofen. "Take this. Drink all the Gatorade."

Lucy knew better than to hesitate. She'd likely pushed him to the end of his patience. Rycks might have taken care with her after the kind of stunt she'd pulled last night, but he'd definitely have no tolerance for her shirking her duties. She doubted Vicious would any better.

"What time is it?"

"Eleven? Didn't look before I came over here."

"Oh, shit! Eleven? I've got to get to the kitchen!" She jumped up, and her stomach promptly heaved. Eyes wide, she looked up at Vicious before sprinting to the bathroom, skidding to a stop on her knees just before she threw up. The scent of whisky and beer combined with sour bile made her even sicker. Lucy was violently ill for several minutes, her grip on the toilet so tight it was a wonder she didn't crack the porcelain. Sweat stood out on her brow, dripping into her eyes as she was sick over and over again.

Gradually, her stomach calmed down, and she collapsed back on her ass on the floor. A wet washcloth appeared in front of her face, and she took it gratefully. That was when she realized his arm was around her, rubbing her arm soothingly.

"Gotta watch that first step, baby."

Despite herself, Lucy chuckled. "Yeah. Figured that one out. I still need to get to the kitchen. Thorn will be pissed and take away my job before I get the chance to do it."

"I told you I'd take care of you, baby. Thorn's good. You start tomorrow."

"I did this to myself. Why'd you bother?" She still felt shaky, and her voice reflected that. Tears still streamed down her cheeks though she was getting better control. The cool cloth he'd given her felt like heaven as she ran it over her face and neck.

"You didn't do it all. The girls were testing you."

"I know that." She sighed. "Went through the same thing at Black Reign. It's a no-win test. I thought I could pace myself, but they made sure there was always a drink in my hand and a reason to down it quickly."

"Well, if it's any consolation, you put them all in their place. Every single one of them got laid last night, but not for the reasons they wanted to."

"Great. That makes me feel *so* much better, Vicious." She started to get up, but he held her down, chuckling.

"Calm down. I'm just sayin' I guarantee the girls' actions backfired on them. Ain't no reason to fear the guys. No one's gonna do anything to you."

"I'm so fucked."

"Here." He handed her the bottle of Gatorade he'd brought for her earlier. "If you think you can keep it down."

"Yeah. Just moved too fast." She sipped several times before taking a larger drink.

"Better?"

"I'm good." Was she? Maybe. Oh, well. *What's done is done*. She'd just have to move forward and put it behind her. If the women let her.

"Uh-huh." He grinned. "Come on. Let's take some more pills and get something in your stomach."

"Not sure I can handle food."

"Then we'll get you a Bloody Mary or something."

"How about maybe just some V8 juice? I'm never drinking again."

"That's good to know. Maybe my pizza and beer will be safe from sticky fingers."

Lucy couldn't help herself. She let out a small bark of laughter. "Yeah. I'll consider the six-pack off limits. I make no promises about the pizza."

Chapter Six

The next few days passed uneventfully for Lucy. She had a couple hiccups with the meals -- mainly the guys expected hotdogs and hamburgers and nothing else. Once she got them interested in a few other things involving meat, they were all good. They balked at chicken as meat, but she finally won them over. Fish, as long as it was deep fried and accompanied by baked beans, mashed potatoes, and mac and cheese was acceptable as well. Mornings were simple. Coffee mostly. Until the men started rising earlier and earlier, wondering what she could come up with for breakfast.

To her relief, the incident at the bonfire was forgotten quickly. Or, at least, no one seemed to make a big deal out of it. More than one of the women asked where she learned to dance like that, but mostly they just dismissed her. Could have been because, as late as she'd been the next morning, she'd noticed every single one of the other women was missing until nearly suppertime. Apparently, the sex had been quite vigorous and plentiful the night before.

Vicious had kept to himself except at night. Then, he was the one dragging her to his room. He insisted they get ready for bed together, and he always made a point to kiss her the second they were in his room. Sometimes, he did so where everyone could see them, but she figured that was all part of the act. Also, not only did he insist they sleep together, but he insisted they... *cuddle*. He always looked so disgruntled about it, but when she called him out, he just grunted and pulled her closer. Always, *always*, his very hard cock was mashed between the cheeks of her ass. Had she not been attracted to him she might have objected. Hell, even if she wasn't attracted to him she might have allowed it because it felt that good. She'd never slept with anyone other than her sister. Then, it was mostly her dozing and watching over Mae. Not really sleeping. What she had with Vicious now felt amazing. Logically, she knew he didn't feel the same way. This was the first time she'd ever had anything like this in her life, and naturally she'd latched on to the big biker. But she'd take what she could get as long as she could get it.

"Not gonna be back tonight, Lucy." Vicious stood at the closet. He'd just zipped up his backpack and shouldered it when she'd entered the room. "I'll try to call you later if I can. If not, you stay here until I get back."

"But I have to do breakfast --"

"Stay. Here." His voice brooked no argument. "Don't leave this room until I come for you."

"Am I in danger?"

"No."

"Then I don't see --"

"Just do what I tell you, girl," he snapped. This wasn't like him at all. He'd never spoken to her harshly other than that first time he'd met her. Even that wasn't like this. "You're in my house. You follow my rules." He wasn't exactly cruel sounding, but she knew better than to argue with him. The contrast between his tenderness at night and the coldness with which he treated her during the day and now was disconcerting. This Vicious she wasn't necessarily afraid of, but she knew to proceed with caution when dealing with him.

For long moments she just looked at him. When she could find her voice, she asked, "Have I done something wrong?"

"No," he said immediately, turning back to the closet to grab a few more items and stuff them in the various pockets of his cargo pants and vest.

"Fine," she said, turning to the bathroom to get dressed for bed. She shut the door more firmly than strictly necessary, but damn it, he'd pissed her off. Worse, this distance hurt her. Which pissed her off even more because she knew better than to care about him in the first damned place.

Once dressed, she reached for the door handle only to have the door open before she could. Vicious stood there, dressed in black. Grease paint even streaked his cheeks as if for camouflage. She had no idea what else it could be for.

Instead of saying anything, she gave him a quick glance then moved past him into the room. If he was going to act like an ass, she'd ignore him. She went to the small table he'd set up for her personal space. Sitting down, she took her hairbrush and began to work through her hair. The curls were always difficult on the best of days, but, strangely, the ritual of ridding herself of the tangles calmed her mind. She closed her eyes and concentrated on her task.

Lucy felt a gentle hand on her shoulder but refused to acknowledge it. The touch was so at odds with the gruff way Vicious had spoken to her she wondered if maybe there was someone else in the room. But over the past few days, she'd learned his touch. His scent. There was no mistaking the man behind her.

"I'm sorry." His gruff apology was simple, but she knew he meant it. Didn't mean she was ready to let him off the hook.

"It's fine." She continued to pull the brush slowly through her hair even as she shrugged her indifference.

"Look at me, Lucy."

"Nothing to apologize for. You got your business. I'll just stay here and deal with mine."

"I can't tell you what's goin' on, but it's important."

"I told you it's fine. You don't have to explain anything to me."

He gave a frustrated sigh. "Just… don't leave this room."

"Already got that," she bit out, sharper than she should have, but this was getting old. Also, the dual personalities bit was getting to her. Messing with her head. "Just get done what you have to so I can get to work. I don't want Thorn kicking me out for not pulling my weight."

She almost felt bad for leaving it at that, but really. What was there to say?

With a heavy sigh, Vicious dropped his hand. She heard his footfalls headed away from her, then he opened and shut the door. It was all Lucy could do not to cry. She wanted the tender man who held her each night. The man who'd saved her from herself and promised to get her sister back. It was time to face facts. It was entirely possible that man was nothing more than a fairytale.

* * *

"All set?" Thorn looked at the group from Salvation's Bane getting ready for the extraction. Vicious had seen that look enough times to know the man was going over every last detail in his head one last time before putting the plan into action. Tonight, they'd bring Mae back to Lucy. Hopefully, with no one the wiser. Vicious had hated keeping this from Lucy, but no one but the team was to know what was going on. This was to be done in strict secrecy. Because Mae was being held in the home of a prominent resident of Palm Beach, on orders from someone in his corporate office. Thing was, both Data and Ripper were convinced the buck didn't stop there. Someone was pulling the strings. Someone bigger and related to Rush Developments.

"Ready, brother," Red answered. As road captain, he was in charge of the move. Their backup and mechanic if anything went awry was Grease. He had the chase vehicle already set up close to their mark. If they needed out in a hurry, he had diversions set up to create a spectacle big enough to draw a crowd from three counties over. It would likely draw law enforcement, so they'd have to move fast, but then, that was what diversions were for. To let them move fast.

"Ripper has already hacked into the security system. He's just waiting for the word from us to flip the switch. Once he does, we'll have fifteen minutes to get in, get the girl, and get out. Do not deviate from that plan. When I say time's up, we pull the plug. Whether or not we have the girl. No one is gettin' caught in this mess."

Vicious wanted to protest but knew better. This was why Thorn was president. He always had the club's best interest at heart. If it got too personal, he stepped back and let Havoc take over. Tonight, it was Thorn, Vicious, Red, and Grease. Ripper was on intel back at the clubhouse. Grease was basically the lookout, and Vicious and Red the team going in. Which left Thorn leading it all and backing up Grease if necessary. Beast, the club's enforcer, was at the clubhouse monitoring everything with Ripper and making sure the clubhouse and everyone inside was secure. No one left tonight. No matter what.

They took the bikes to within a mile of the estate where Mae was being held. From there, Grease and Red took them in a big Humvee to just outside the perimeter of the estate. They were just about to call Ripper when they heard a second vehicle approaching. And it sounded like a bike. A fast bike.

"Goddamn," Thorn swore. "That better not be who the fuck I think it is."

A matte-black Ninja H2R pulled up next to the Humvee. The man on it was dressed in black leather with a black full-face helmet. Under normal circumstances, Vicious would have made fun of the crotch rocket, but all he felt now was rage. If they'd been played, Vicious was going to beat the fuck out of the entire Black Reign club. Starting with the motherfucker getting off that Goddamned bike.

"Rycks," Thorn said, stepping toward the other man. "I swear by God and sunny Jesus, if you've fucked us over I'm gonna slit your Goddamned throat right here."

"Of course it's Rycks," Vicious muttered. "What tie do you have to Mae?" he demanded the second Rycks's helmet was off. "Why are you here?"

"Mae is... special."

"El Diablo agreed that if we pull this off, Mae comes with us. You goin' against your president?"

"Not at all," Rycks said. "But I'll make sure she's safely away."

Red spat on the ground. "Don't trust that motherfucker. Or his rat-ass, piece of shit bike."

"It's the fastest bike on the road. We need a quick getaway, I can get her out."

"Not that a fuckin' Ninja isn't noticeable or anything," Vicious said. "Girl comes with us."

"Let her decide. Either way, she'll go back to your compound. I just want to make sure she's safe." Rycks wasn't giving an inch. This wasn't going to be easy.

Looking at Thorn, Vicious could see the other man running through the possibilities. Deciding which option to was more likely to bring them the outcome they wanted.

"Fine. You come with us." He stepped toward Rycks until they were nose to nose. "But if you do anything to jeopardize my team or our ability to rescue that girl, you'll be the first of many to die."

"Understood," Rycks answered without hesitation. "I just want her safe."

Thorn held his gaze for several seconds. Neither man blinking or backing down an inch. "What's she to you?"

Rycks shrugged. "Does it matter?"

Thorn snorted, turning away from him. "Is everything in place?" He addressed Red.

The big man nodded. "Just waiting your word. Ripper's ready to go."

Thorn turned back to Ryker. "Once we give the word and Ripper disables the security system we'll have fifteen minutes to get in and get her out. We have to be outside the estate grounds. If we run out of time, we leave. I will not risk my brothers. No negotiation."

Rycks raised his hands as if in surrender. "I follow your lead. I'm merely here to help."

"Right," Vicious muttered. "And I'm Mother Teresa." Thorn gave him a quelling glance. "Come on, Thorn. Are we really doing this?"

"Man's got a reason to be here. Better to have him where we can watch him."

The members of Salvation's Bane looked around uneasily. It was rare anyone spoke against their president. And never in front of another club.

"No harm meant, Thorn. I just want Lucy's sister back safely."

"Understandable, brother." Thorn clapped him on the shoulder. "All right boys. Let's do this."

* * *

The estate was about three acres surrounded by a wrought iron fence. Two sides faced the road, two sides were wooded acreage that acted as a buffer between houses. Thankfully, there were several of these natural barriers throughout the upscale neighborhood for added privacy. Those wooded areas would be their escape route. Seemed pretty straightforward to Vicious. Not that he was expecting much. This guy wasn't exactly hard core. He was an investment banker. There was the expected security plus two security guards. The main thing they were worried about was the floodlights. If they cut them, it was a dead giveaway for an alert guard. So they had to maneuver around them in the shadows.

"Last proof of life showed the girl smiling while riding a horse," Red said. "Hopefully, that's a good indicator she's been treated well."

"Agreed, brother," Vicious said. Rycks simply studied the estate and the route they'd laid out at Thorn's instructions.

"Where's the stable?" Rycks asked.

"There isn't one." Thorn answered. "Probably took her someplace away from the estate. She's obviously not in distress in that photo."

"Hmmm."

"Well, you're obviously not impressed, Rycks." Vicious didn't like the man, but he respected him. If there was something they were overlooking, he wanted to know sooner rather than later.

"Don't know. Do we know when the photo they sent us was taken?"

"Only by time stamp," Thorn said. Rycks had his full attention now by the look of him. "Didn't have Ripper or Data look into it too far. You think I should have?"

"Not sure," Ripper said, continuing to study the layout, looking over the terrain before them from time to time. Probably to get his bearings and an idea of where he was going. "What was the time stamp?"

"A week ago."

"To the day?"

Thorn nodded slowly. "Today's Wednesday. Stamp said Thursday the previous week."

"Hum." Rycks's gaze landed on Thorn. "Picture was sunny. Bright. She was smiling, but her eyes were squinted, and the trees had dark shadows on the ground."

"Yeah," Thorn said, his face going hard. "The day it was supposed to have been taken was one of the hardest rains we've had all year. All fuckin' day." Thorn swore as he holstered his gun. Not his normal piece. They were all armed with tranq guns and beanbag rifles. They weren't there to kill anyone. Just secure the girl and get out. Not only would the sound of gunfire in such a neighborhood draw vast amounts of unwanted attention, but having dead bodies turn up in one of the most prominent neighborhoods in Palm Beach would just scream "investigation."

"Don't mean she's not still fine." Vicious tried to judge Thorn's next decision, but had no idea what it would be. He saw no reason to deviate from the original plan.

"No. But she might not be in as good a shape as we've been lead to believe." He nodded to Rycks. "Might be glad you're with us if we have to carry her out. You're the only one of use she knows. Would she fight you if she thought she was in danger?"

"No. I've never harmed Mae. I *would* never harm her. We had a contentious relationship out of necessity, but I've never done anything to let her think I'd hurt her."

"She don't know us. Seeing a familiar face might be the thing that gets her out of there quietly."

"Understood," Rycks said, holstering his own tranq gun. "I'd feel better with at least one pistol with real ammunition."

"Can't risk it," Thorn said without hesitation. "We think we need that kind of firepower, we abort. Ain't riskin' anybody, and ain't riskin' the club." Vicious glanced at Rycks to find the other man meeting his gaze. Thorn must have seen it too because he added, "Anyone goes against me, I'll shoot you myself." His tone of voice said he absolutely meant it. "Let's move."

Getting to the house proved less difficult than Vicious would have thought. They saw one guard who was pretty alert, but just not able to take in the whole grounds by himself. He was in regular contact with his counterpart, though, from what Ripper could tell, not at any set time. He'd been watching the place for three days. The guards checked in anywhere from five to ten minutes from the top and bottom of the hour. Which gave them their fifteen-minute window when Ripper dropped the security system. He had camera feeds to loop during their entry and exit so whoever was manning the cameras shouldn't be the wiser, and any motion sensors would be switched off.

"Don't see no obvious surprises," Red said, filling Thorn and Ripper in on what was happening on the ground. "We good?"

"You'll be good to go fifteen seconds after the guard's next transmission. I'll give you a countdown," came Ripper's voice over the earpiece. "Be ready on my mark."

There was a churning in Vicious's gut that shouldn't be there. This was nothing compared to the missions he'd run with ExFil, the company run by Bones's president, Cain. They were mercenaries who went all over the world into some of the most dangerous situations and he was getting nervous over an extraction in his own city? That was some bullshit right there.

He glanced at Red. The man's face was an emotionless mask. Hard to say if he was bothered by it, but Rycks... Rycks checked and rechecked his weapon, paying special attention to the knife strapped to his thigh. They weren't supposed to have live ammunition, but every one of them carried a knife. Wasn't that they expected to use it to defend themselves, but sometimes a knife came in handy under any circumstance. Bottom line, Rycks was nervous, or anxious. It was possible the man wasn't used to fighting or combat, but Vicious didn't think so. Rycks struck him as calm and capable. He wouldn't be in El Diablo's inner circle if he were a shrinking violet.

"Fifteen seconds." Ripper's voice over the earpiece brought Vicious abruptly back to the situation at hand. "Ten seconds." He scanned the area. They already had their route planned from blueprints of the house Ripper had obtained. Now, they executed the plan efficiently, and they would be out in less than fifteen minutes. "Five, four, three, two, one, mark."

The three of them entered through the poolside entrance. The owner of the house was in his study, so they had easy access through the door closest to where they believe Mae was being held. Thorn and Grease would be spotting them from a distance, as well as Ripper keeping an eye on them via the camera links.

"I see you," Ripper said. "Way's clear to the end of the hall."

The crouched as they moved. Vicious was grateful the guy had minimal security, though he wondered about that. Either he didn't feel the need for anything heavier because he had no anticipation anyone would come for the girl, or he'd just never done anything like this before and wasn't prepared.

"Second floor, third door on the left. That's where she should be. You've got thirteen minutes left. Still all clear."

"Where's the guy's wife?" Rycks asked softly. "The kids?"

"Wife's out of town. Kids'r at a summer camp, according to the texts he's exchanged with them. Probably planned both around this kidnapping."

Rycks only grunted. They didn't stop moving until they reached the room in question. Red picked the lock quietly while Vicious kept a look out. Rycks alternately kept an eye out with Vicious and watched Red, obviously anxious to get inside the room.

The second the door was open, Rycks entered. There was only one light coming from the bathroom. There was no furniture, and the floor was a bare, hardwood laminate. A small whimper sounded, and

Rycks was on the move. It took a moment for Vicious to see what Rycks had already spotted. A small figure huddled in the corner next to the bathroom. As he approached, she released a sound much like that of a wounded animal anticipating another blow. It was then Vicious realized this little creature was Lucy's sister, Mae.

It was hard to tell in the dim lighting, but she was dressed only in her underwear and was filthy. The room was spotless, so she had to have been moved here recently. A length of chain was fastened to her ankle, the other end bolted into the floor. Looked like she had enough room to get to the toilet but not much else.

"It's me, Mae," Rycks tried to soothe the girl, but she still cowered in the corner, whimpering pathetically. "It's Rycks."

It didn't seem to help. He reached for her ankle to let Red pick the handcuff, and she shrieked, kicking out at him even as she tried to scoot farther into the corner.

"Damn it, girl. Stop!" Rycks didn't yell at her, but his voice was decidedly firmer. "It's Rycks. You know I'm not gonna hurt you. Settle down." Surprisingly, she did. She still whimpered, but she let him have her ankle while Red freed her.

Vicious quickly examined her. "We may have a problem, Thorn. She's hurt and traumatized. Not sure she can make it out on her own power."

"I can carry her," Rycks said immediately. "Just need these guys to cover my back and I'll get her out."

"Whatever works," Thorn said. "Ripper? Time."

"Seven minutes, thirteen seconds."

"Get it done," Thorn ordered. "We'll be ready when you get out."

"She'll need clothes," Rycks said as he pulled off his T-shirt and put it over her head. "Bastards had her in her underwear."

"Not important," Thorn snapped. "Get back here without being seen. Get her to the clubhouse."

"On it. Depart in ten seconds," Red said as he worked the lock on the cuff until it released. "Go!"

Rycks scooped Mae up, and the three of them headed back down the hall the way they came. Still, the place was eerily silent. The only people around seemed to be the two guards.

They made it to the sunroom and poolside entrance, crouching in the shadows. "We're just inside the house. Ready to exit on your call."

"The second guard joined the first," Ripper said. Though he sounded calm, there was a note of anxiety in his voice. "They're too close for you to get away clean."

"How much time?" That was from Thorn. "Got to be getting close."

"Four minutes before it resets automatically. Understand, the only way to prevent it is to cut power to the whole house, and that would be a dead giveaway."

"Give it a couple more minutes," Thorn said. "If they haven't moved, we'll reevaluate."

Mae still whimpered occasionally, but otherwise lay passively in Rycks's arms. The big man's face was hard, angry. No doubt he wanted to kill someone. Vicious could understand. He was itching to do some smashing, too.

"They're not moving," Ripper said, now showing his anxiety. "We're gonna have to do something different."

"Just relax," Thorn said. "Give it a couple more seconds."

"Seventy-three seconds," Ripper said. "Seventy." There was a beat of silence. "If I'm gonna cut the power I need to do it in the next thirty seconds."

"Can you do it for the whole neighborhood?"

"No. I wasn't prepared for that. I don't have that kind of grid access, and it would take too long to get it."

"They're moving!" Thorn said. "Give it a second."

"They're going east of the house," Ripper said. "Just rounding the corner. Go! Now! Go!"

They opened the door and sprinted across the yard. Vicious made sure to close the door so when the security system came on there wasn't a breach detected.

"Fifteen seconds," Ripper continued his countdown. "You have to get to the tree line and out of range of the cameras!"

"Got that," Red bit out.

"Eight seconds. Five!"

Just as he called out engagement of the security system, they crossed into the woods. They didn't slow down, but kept running as quickly as they dared. They didn't want to sound like a herd of buffalo but needed to get back to the group.

"Stop, stop!" Vicious hissed softly, knowing the throat mike would catch his words. "Get down!"

Just ahead of them was a group of four men, moving like military. They were armed with what looked like M-16s and held them like they knew how to use them.

"Fuck," Red hissed. "Four bogies in our path. Thorn, can you see them?"

"Negative. I've got no visual."

"Due south of you. Just below that little knoll above the grounds. We're in the dip just below them."

There was a short silence before Thorn finally said, "Got 'em." Then another silence. "Fuck." Finally he said, "Military. No markings. Tranq 'em."

The second the words left Thorn's mouth, Red and Vicious fired at the same time, each hitting a man in the thigh. It took several seconds for the drugs to take effect , so they followed up with beanbags. Thorn and Grease fired as well, hitting each man with multiple darts. It still took nearly thirty seconds for the four to go down. Unfortunately, one of them got off a radio transmission.

"Oh, shit! Get out of there, guys," Ripper yelled. "There's more of them, and I have no idea how many! Get out now!"

"Calm the fuck down, Ripper," Thorn ordered calmly. "Can you make it, Vicious?"

He glanced at Rycks and Mae. The man was talking softly to Mae, who appeared to still be in a catatonic state. She'd mostly stopped whimpering, but showed no signs of coming back to the world around her.

"Rycks," he called. "You good? We need to go now."

"I've got her. Let's go."

Rycks scooped Mae over his shoulder in a fireman's carry. The girl wasn't big as a minute so it wouldn't have been hard to just carry her out. Rycks, like Vicious, probably believed there were more waiting for them and wanted to keep his hands free.

The men moved from their cover deeper into the woods. They were about five hundred yards away from Grease and Thorn. Didn't seem like far, but when faced with an unknown number of enemies, Vicious felt like it was trying to reach the fucking moon.

He thought he could just make out the Humvee about a hundred yards out when two men shot out of the trees and landed heavily. One directly on Red, the other just missing Vicious. The assailants came at them with knives, their intent to kill. Vicious felt the bite of a blade graze his shoulder as he spun away. Conscious of the fact that Rycks would be hampered with Mae, he did his best to keep his body between his attacker and that of the other man and the girl.

A ferocious fight began as another man joined in. They were too close to use the beanbags or the tranq guns, so Vicious grabbed a dart from his belt and stabbed it into the leg of his attacker. Still they fought, taking precious seconds before the effect even started to slow the big guy down. Vicious heard Red swear as he fought his guy from his position on the ground, kicking out and throwing the guy back over his head against a nearby tree. The big man merely shook his head before climbing to his feet and launching himself at Red once again.

Rycks had two darts in hand and stabbed his attacker in the shoulder once, then in the side of the neck. The neck shot got the guy to stumble back, and Rycks took advantage, kicking out and knocking the guy into a tree.

Just as Vicious thought his team had the upper hand, Thorn came over the radio. "Three more on you in ten."

"We're not gonna be able to get out of here without killin' someone, Thorn," Vicious admitted. "These guys are going for the kill. This is some real bullshit right here."

"Take 'em out. We're on our way to you."

That was all the permission Vicious needed. Ten seconds later, three guys burst from the dark. He pulled his knife and went to work.

Chapter Seven

Bloodbath.

If ever the term applied, it was now. Vicious got the first guy on him in the side of the neck, stabbing several times in rapid succession. The next guy was ready for him, going low, trying to catch Vicious in the thigh. He twisted away and stabbed the attacker in the side under his armpit just above his vest. He and Red were mindful of Rycks with their small, frightened charge and did their best to keep themselves between the other man and the oncoming bogies.

He should have known Rycks wouldn't hunker down with Mae. He put her on her side against the tree and covered her with his vest. Fucker left himself wide open with no protection. Apparently, Rycks was hoping their attackers didn't have the same scruples as Bane did about using guns so the whole fucking neighborhood wouldn't hear them. Well, he'd be shit outta luck if anyone had suppressed firepower. Hell. With this many hostiles, they all would.

More and more men came at them until all three of them were covered in blood from the elbows down. The ground around them was littered with bodies and still more came at them.

"Guy has a fuckin' army!" Red muttered as he slammed a knife into the throat of a guy he'd just body slammed to the ground. "Investment banker my fuckin' ass."

"Didn't come from the investment banker, dumbass." Rycks grunted as another guy attacked him. He went low, slashing deep in a diagonal up the guy's inner thigh before stabbing under his armpit several times in brutal thrusts.

"I'll kill you myself if you've held back from us," Thorn's voice came over the radio almost on top of the clipped *snap snap* of a suppressed rifle. That would be Thorn's group. The two guys closest to Vicious and Red dropped. Both of them clean head shots.

"Not holdin' back. You guys knew this guy was a middleman." Rycks jumped on the next attacker, pulled back his head and slid his knife smoothly and deeply across the guy's throat. Blood spurted when he hit the artery, arcing through the air and onto the ground.

Two more shots took out two more attackers while Red and Vicious took the last two. They stood there several seconds, catching their breath and making sure there were no more sleepers.

"We're too exposed here," he muttered. They had no battle helmets and weren't protected at all from head shots -- even a whack to the head. If there was a sniper out there -- and they'd be foolish to believe there wasn't -- they were sitting ducks.

"She OK?" Red asked Rycks. Mae hadn't made a sound, still huddled under Rycks's vest. The big man was crouched above the girl, coaxing her to sit and look at him.

"Still in shock," he muttered. "We've got to get her out of here. Now."

When he stood, Vicious could see Rycks covered in blood across his torso. Looked like most of it wasn't his own, but he had numerous scratches and deeper lacerations over his chest and arms. A couple on his face as well.

"Way's clear," Thorn said. "We're just ahead of you. Get back to the cage. We'll cover you."

"Might want to send in a cleaner," Vicious snarled as he picked up Rycks's vest and hurried after him and the girl. "Left a fuckin' mess down here."

"Already on the way." That was Ripper. "Havoc and Beast are gettin' a team together. I've jammed 9-1-1 calls from this area, but so far no one seems to be the wiser. Should have the place spick and span by morning."

"Good," Thorn said. "Make sure they don't leave the clubhouse unprotected. Don't want these bastards coming after us."

"Got it covered."

Ten minutes later, they were at the drop-off site, cleaning blood off them as best they could. Thankfully, they always had a change of clothing packed for everyone just in case something went sideways.

They didn't have much for Mae. A pair of sweats and socks to go with Rycks's shirt was about all they could manage. Rycks was talking to her quietly. She stood on her feet, her arms wrapped around herself. That she was standing on her own was a good sign, Vicious thought. When Rycks put a helmet on her, though, Vicious shook his head.

"Not happening, Rycks. She rides in the cage with us."

Rycks didn't acknowledge him, just continued to speak softly to Mae as he threaded her arms through his leather jacket. No patch, naturally. They didn't want to be identified.

"Put her in the truck. Now."

Mae whimpered at his tone and flinched back. Rycks put his hands on her shoulders gently, bending down so he could look at her face. When he stood, he ushered her to his bike. "I'm taking her back with me."

"Like fuckin' hell," Vicious snapped. "The deal was, we do this, she comes with us. Lucy wants her sister back."

Rycks turned on him, advancing. There was no doubt he was ready to fight over this. A fight just as brutal and bloody as the one they were just in. "That was before I saw how traumatized she is."

"And you think Black Reign is the best place for her?"

"I do. She'll feel safe there."

Thorn shut the tailgate of the truck and pulled the top down. "Didn't she get taken from the Black Reign compound?"

There was silence. A muscle in Rycks's jaw ticked.

"Yeah. Put her in the fuckin' truck. Tell El Diablo she's safe and get your ass back where you belong."

"I'm not leaving her." The steel in his voice matched Thorn's.

"Follow if you want. But you ain't gettin' in our house. You weren't invited to this party."

"You needed me, Thorn. Still do."

"No. I don't. Any help you could have given came before all this happened. Had you told us more about what we were facing, we might have come up with a better plan."

"I was under orders not to!" He sounded like he was becoming desperate. "Look. These people are the most dangerous I've ever met. El Diablo was high in their ranks before he left, El Segador a top-level enforcer. Both international. It's why El Diablo didn't come for his daughter sooner. When they left, both knew there would be repercussions. They are trying to keep those to a minimum for everyone's sake."

"Ain't got time for this," Thorn said as he strode toward Mae and Rycks, pulling his gun as he went. "Get her in the truck. Now. You don't, I kill you and do it myself. One more body ain't gonna mean nothing to me at this point."

Vicious knew Thorn would do it, too. Kill Rycks and to hell with the whole of Black Reign. After holding his gaze for several moments, Rycks finally turned back to Mae and removed the helmet.

"These men are going to take you to Lucy. I need you to go with them."

Mae whimpered, her whole body starting to tremble again. With a sigh, Rycks picked her up in his arms and carried her to the truck, setting her in the middle of the back seat and fastening her seat belt.

Vicious thought he heard Mae whimper, "Please don't leave me, Rycks. I'll be good. What you tell me." The big man didn't answer her. Just cupped her face gently before pressing a kiss to the top of her head.

"Anything more happens to her, you will answer to me," he said, meeting Thorn's gaze. "Only reason I'm agreeing to this is I'm not at all certain I can safely keep her on the bike."

"She's ours to protect, Rycks," Vicious snarled. "Lucy's family is my family. You're the one who let this happen in the first place."

For the briefest moment, Rycks looked... devastated? There was a pain so deep Vicious might have only imagined he saw it. It was obvious he cared for the girl in some way, but it was hard to determine his relationship with Mae. He'd been gentle with her, but like that of a guardian. Not of a lover. Which was good. Mae was only seventeen. If he'd claimed the girl that way, Vicious would have to kill him.

"Believe me, Vicious," he said quietly. "No one is more aware of that than I." Rycks turned and got on his bike, starting it up and speeding off into the night.

"We gotta move," Thorn said.

Vicious got in the truck beside Mae, careful to keep his movements slow so he didn't startle the already terrified girl. "Everything's gonna be all right," Vicious told her as they sped off. "I'm gonna get you to Lucy, and everything will be good."

"No, it won't," Mae surprised him by saying softly. "Nothing will ever be good again." Had he not been a badass, that might have broken his heart. As it was, Vicious merely grunted, patting her hand awkwardly.

* * *

The soft knock at her door brought Lucy out of a fitful sleep. She'd broken down slightly after Vicious had left. She'd shed a few tears but, really, what was there to cry over? It wasn't like they had a chance at a happily ever after. He was protecting her, like she'd wanted, until they found her sister. Then it was over. They'd leave. She had no idea where they'd go, but they couldn't stay with either club. Black Reign didn't care about them, and Salvation's Bane was too close to Vicious. Because, once this was done, she knew he'd move on.

She opened the door and found Thorn there. "Hi," she said inanely.

"You look tired," he said with a concerned expression. Looked like he was a bit uncomfortable being there. "You OK?"

"Fine. What's up?" She knew she sounded clipped, but she'd learned that was really the only way to deal with bikers.

"We got your sister," he said softly.

"Oh my God, really? Is she OK?"

He hesitated. "She's been traumatized, Lucy. I have no idea how or what exactly was done to her, but she needs care."

"Where is she?" She stepped out of the room.

"I'll take you."

"Wait," she put a hand on his arm. "Where's Vicious? Did he help?"

"He did. I think he and Red are cleaning up and taking care of their wounds. I'm sure he'll come get you later."

"Wounds? Oh, God! What happened?" She was becoming alarmed. She knew her sister needed her, but did Vicious need her, too? And what would she do if he did? She couldn't abandon her sister, and it sounded like Mae needed her more than she ever had.

"Ran into trouble we didn't expect. Fortunately, Rycks insisted on joining the party and they had help they wouldn't have. Still wasn't pretty, but that's not for you. Let me take you to your sister."

"Rycks."

Thorn just grunted.

He led her to a room two doors down and opened it. Inside, in a bed on the far side of the room away from the windows, Mae was under several layers of quilts, curled in a ball. Her eyes were open, and she stared at Lucy in wide-eyed fear for a few seconds until she finally realized who was in the room with her. Thorn laid a gentle hand on Lucy's shoulder.

"She's been through more than we'd first thought. Rycks was the only one she responded to. She didn't want him to leave her." Thorn sighed before adding, "He wanted to take her back to Black Reign, but we wouldn't let him. I know you want Mae with you, but I'm not sure that it's not a good idea. At least until she heals."

Lucy winced. This was it. He was going to kick them out. Better to do it now than to wait around until she was so attached to Vicious it ripped out her heart.

"Let me look her over. As soon as she can make it comfortably, I'd appreciate it if you could give us a ride back. Assuming El Diablo lets us back."

"I honestly don't think Rycks will have it any other way."

"Rycks was always protective of her, but they were constantly at each other. He belittled her, but she gave it right back to him. I don't understand why he'd want us back."

"Lucy," Thorn said, hesitating before he continued. "He didn't say both of you. He wants Mae. I don't think he'd object if you wanted to come with her, but he's not as insistent. His focus is Mae. She's not… responded well since he left."

Lucy let out a sob before she could rein it in. "She's my baby sister. I promised I'd take care of her. Look out for her."

"This isn't your fault, Lucy," Thorn offered gently. "What we ran up against… you're damned lucky you weren't around when she was taken."

Brushing away tears, she stepped into the room and crossed to the bed. Mae's eyes never strayed from hers, but she didn't move or say anything. Lucy sat on the bed. When she reached over to brush a lock of matted hair out of her sister's face, Mae flinched back. Lucy felt it like a solid slap.

"I'm so sorry, Mae. I promised I'd keep you safe, and I couldn't." No response. "Thorn said Rycks wants us to come back to Black Reign." Mae shifted but said nothing. "Do you want him to come get us?" Her sister didn't speak, but, after a moment, nodded her head slightly. "I'll tell Thorn. Once you're able to move, they'll take us back." Again, Mae said nothing nor acknowledged her in any way. "Get some rest. Once you feel like it, we'll get you up and get you a nice long, hot bath. I'll wash your hair and get all the tangles out of it. How would that be?" No response.

Lucy was becoming desperate but dared not push Mae any further. She needed sleep. And time. Neither looked like they would be easily given.

Chapter Eight

"I can't believe you're lettin' that mother fucker in here." Vicious paced the common room like a lion on the prowl. He hated the idea of having Rycks in Bane territory at all, much less in their fucking clubhouse.

"It's not about what I want," Thorn responded softly. "It's about what Mae needs. He's been the only one she's responded to. I was there when Lucy asked if she wanted to go back to Reign. For whatever reason, despite their outward relationship, she trusts him. More than anything, she needs to be with someone she trusts right now."

"You sayin' she don't trust Lucy? Cause I won't believe it. Lucy loves her sister more than anything."

"I'm sayin' she's got some kind of bond with Rycks. Same as he has with her. Mae needs to be with him." One thing Thorn was good at was reading people. It's why they all followed him so easily when every man in Bane was as dominant as they came. If he said Mae needed to be with Rycks, then that was where she needed to go.

"Fine. Don't mean I have to like him comin' around."

"Lucy intends to go with them." Thorn didn't pull any punches.

Vicious's head whipped around and he glared at Thorn. "No fuckin' way."

"Not my decision, brother. Lucy doesn't want to leave her sister." Vicious noted Thorn didn't add his opinion on that.

All of a sudden, the room didn't have enough air. Vicious's chest felt heavy, and his heart raced. No way he was letting her leave. Especially not to go back to Black Reign.

"Like bloody hell," he grumbled, then stomped away to find Lucy.

As expected, she was in Mae's room, sitting beside the bed. Mae's small hand was in Lucy's, but Mae didn't acknowledge Lucy other than to glance up at her from time to time as if for reassurance. She did so when she became aware of Vicious. Yeah. No doubt the girl needed to be somewhere she felt safe, and Bane wasn't it.

Vicious went to Lucy and placed a hand on her shoulder. Lucy looked up at him. "We need to talk." Vicious tried not to be gruff about it, but didn't seem to be able to rein it in. He was not letting her go. If he had to tie her to his bed he would.

"I can't leave Mae," Lucy said, looking away from him. "She needs me."

"No one's gonna hurt her here. You know that, right?"

"I know, but she's frightened."

Thorn knocked lightly on the open door, not entering until Lucy acknowledged him. "I'll sit with her if you like," he said, his voice soft and sincere. "I know the two of you have some things to work out."

Lucy looked from Thorn to Vicious, then back to Mae. Mae had closed her eyes and lay passively. "I guess we need to." She looked at Thorn. "She wants to go with Rycks."

"I know. I've already contacted him. He'll be here in a few minutes to take her back to Lake Worth."

Lucy gasped and ducked her head. Her slim shoulders rose and fell as her breathing quickened. "I guess we better make it quick." She didn't look at Vicious.

Mae's hand was limp as Lucy removed hers and gently tucked her sister's arm back under the covers. At some point during the last day, Lucy had managed to wash Mae's hair. Long, dark hair much like Lucy's spilled out over the pillow in a soft fall. She looked so small and vulnerable. Vicious understood Lucy's reluctance to leave her.

He held out his hand to Lucy, and she took it immediately. At least she wasn't rejecting him completely.

Once in his room, he pulled her into his arms. She was stiff at first, but the longer he held her, the more she relaxed. She took a shuddering breath, then she let go.

Great sobs were torn from Lucy. Grief like Vicious had rarely seen in his life, even on the battlefield, seemed to tear through her like a firestorm. It was like the stress of the last few months with her sister was finally coming to a head. She cried for a good fifteen minutes, the dam bursting right before his eyes.

Once she'd worn herself out, Vicious used his shirt tail to wipe her tears. She gave him an incredulous look.

"I'm not wiping my nose on your shirt. That's just gross." She wiggled until he let her up, and she went to the bathroom to clean up. No way Vicious was letting her distance herself from him. He followed her, using the opportunity to change his shirt as he went.

"I'm not good at this," he said, scrubbing his hand over his face. Her tears had nearly ripped out his heart. Not that he was a cold-hearted bastard or anything, but he usually equated women's tears with manipulation. This had been nothing but raw grief, and he wasn't about to insult her by even thinking differently. Besides, he'd let more than one tear slip free himself.

"At what?" She still hadn't met his gaze. Standing in front of the vanity mirror, she washed her face. Vicious stood behind her with his hands on her shoulders.

"I don't… Lucy, I need you to stay here." Her gaze snapped up to collide with his. "With me."

"I can't," she whispered, but Vicious could tell it was more a reflexive response.

"You can. In fact, I insist." When she opened her mouth to protest, Vicious turned her around and gripped her shoulders gently, but firmly. "Look. Your sister needs to be with Rycks. Even you can't deny that. But no one says you have to go as well. We're only ten minutes from them. You can see her any time you want. I'll make sure of it. I need you to stay. With me." He knew he was being repetitive, but he couldn't think beyond those words. He needed her. With him.

She looked at him for a long time. Fresh tears seemed to form, but she blinked them back. "I thought…" She closed her eyes, shaking her head a little. "I thought you were angry with me. Tired of me always being in your way."

"What?" Had she slapped him, he couldn't have been more surprised. "No, baby. Never. Why would you think that?"

"The night you left to go get Mae, you seemed angry at me. I know I probably cramped your style, but I didn't mean to. I would have been all right on my own. You didn't have to shelter me from the other guys."

"You sayin' you wanted other guys hittin' on you? Cause I'm not OK with that."

She blinked. "I don't understand. I thought this was all for show. I actually thought you'd still have women. You did. Right?"

Did she look hurt, or was it just wishful thinking? Did he want her to feel as possessive of him as he was her? Absolutely he did.

Vicious let his hands slide from her shoulders, up her neck, to cup her face gently. "Honey, I've not even looked at another woman since I first saw you. I just didn't want to frighten you off."

She gave a little laugh. "So you forced me to sleep with you at night? In your room?"

He gave her a sheepish grin. "Well, in my defense, you knew that was all bullshit from the start. In any case, I wanted to keep my word to you. I didn't want to do anything you didn't want. I was trying to wait until you came to me."

Lucy gave him a small, watery smile. "I can't abandon Lucy, Vicious. I won't deny I want to stay with you, but my sister needs me." Vicious could see the truth of it in her eyes. She did want him.

He lowered his mouth to hers, kissing her tenderly. He'd done so often, but not since the night he left to rescue Mae. He'd missed her. Terribly.

* * *

Lucy felt like she was being torn apart. More than anything in her life, she wanted to stay with Vicious. Like he said, it was only a ten-minute drive to Lake Worth. Maybe she could come visit him. But that wouldn't be the same, and she knew it. Just as it wouldn't be the same for her to go visit Mae.

Kissing Vicious was always so exciting. Like he was on the very verge of losing himself in her. The thought was a heady aphrodisiac. He was so dominant and demanding, but she knew he'd give her anything she needed in the bedroom simply because she wanted it. Looking back over the time she'd been there, he'd pretty much done anything she wanted out of the bedroom.

He'd protected her from his club and the girls in it, even though she was pretty sure he told the truth when he said none of the men would do anything she didn't want. She'd seen it every single day she was there. They were a rowdy bunch, but they never touched her or did more than ask her to dance for them. OK, so a few of them had actually gotten on their knees and begged, but she could forgive that because they had seemed really sincere and had respected the "no" she'd given them. They'd also made sure to do it in front of Vicious, which made her think it was as much to make him jealous as it was to see if they could get a repeat of the bonfire performance.

His lips tugged and teased at hers, his tongue slipping between her lips. When she opened for him, he swept in and tangled his tongue with hers. There was no way to keep the sigh of contentment and desire contained. She didn't want to. She wanted Vicious. Had from the first moment she'd seen him. He was so larger than life and masculine. His body a work of erotic art. If she could have created the perfect man for her, she'd have created Vicious. She had no idea of his past life, no idea what he'd planned for the future, but she knew she wanted to be with him as long as he'd let her.

"I want you," she whispered. "Now. Before I have to leave."

"Told you," he said between kisses. "Don't want you goin'."

"But Mae --"

"We'll work that out to your satisfaction without you leavin'." He continued to kiss her. "Later."

He pulled back so he could grab the shirt she wore and whip it over her head, leaving only her lacy bra and jeans. The jeans followed the shirt, and Vicious sank to one knee before her. His hands shaped her curves reverently. Soon, his lips followed, kissing her hip bone, her belly button... and lower. As he pulled her panties over her hips to let them pool at her ankles, he continued to kiss until he got to just above her bare pussy. Then he looked up at her, meeting her gaze with his hot one before he thrust his tongue between her folds.

Lucy gasped, grasping his shoulders to keep her balance. When she did, Vicious shouldered his way between her legs and plunged his tongue deep. His deep growl rumbled through her body. Her clit throbbed and twitched with every touch of his lips and tongue. When her knees gave out, he set her on the vanity, spread her legs wide, and buried his face between them.

Bracing her feet on the counter, Lucy grasped Vicious's hair, unsure if she wanted to pull him to her or push him away to get relief from the awful need he was building steadily and terribly within her. She'd known sex with Vicious would be explosive, but this was more than she'd been ready for. There was no doubt she wanted him. Had to have him. But how much of herself was she really ready to cede to this man?

Her answer? *Everything*!

The second she admitted it to herself, her body surrendered to Vicious, letting him take her where he wanted. Which seemed to be straight into madness.

"Oh, yeah, baby," he said in a husky whisper. "That's it. Let yourself go." She obeyed without hesitation, spreading her legs as wide as she could, hooking her hands under her knees to keep them apart. He simply spread her lips wider with his big fingers before carefully inserting one inside her.

Lucy wasn't a virgin, but her experience had been limited. She had always been very careful not to give the impression she was willing to have sex with customers, and when she and Mae had gone to Black Reign, she'd kept her legs firmly closed to the club members. Now, she had no defense. No reason to hold back. She wanted Vicious, no matter the consequences. For the first time in a very long time, she felt like there might be life beyond exotic dancing and paying her father's debts. Maybe, just maybe, there could be a happy ever after for her. It was a dangerous line of thinking, but she couldn't seem to help herself. This was a man she wanted for herself.

"So fuckin' tight," he rasped. "Gonna fuck you soon, Lucy. Gonna put my cock inside you and fuck you 'til you scream."

She was about to *scream* before he fucked her. Just a couple more seconds and she would. He seemed to know she was about to come because he suddenly withdrew his fingers and stood. She opened her mouth to protest, but he covered it with his, kissing her so she tasted herself on his lips. That was so fuckin' hot!

He stepped back from her and dropped his pants and underwear. Once he was naked, he lifted her, urging her to wrap her legs around his waist, and carried her to the bed.

Lucy felt like she was in a fairytale. The pleasure and need building inside her didn't seem real. Women only felt like this in books. Didn't they? She had no assurances from Vicious he wanted more from her than sex. Had no assurances he even wanted her beyond a week or a month. Hell, she'd known him less time than she'd known Rycks, and now she was willing to throw her lot in with him? Yes. Unquestionably, yes. At least, for now.

Once he laid her on the bed, Vicious covered her with his big body, settling himself between her legs. At some point, he'd rolled on a condom, holding up the empty packet so she could see it.

"I look forward to the day when I don't need these with you, Lucy. I don't want nothin' between us." Then he eased inside her.

She gasped. He stretched her until her pussy burned. It wasn't painful, only full and slightly uncomfortable for several seconds. Vicious let her have the time she needed to adjust. Lucy was very conscious of him watching her, of the carefulness with which he moved. She felt him skin to skin with her belly and knew he was inside her as far as he could go. Lucy instinctively raised her legs so her knees hugged his sides. He gave her a sexy grin, then began to... *move*.

The rhythm he set was slow. At first. The more she whimpered and moaned, the faster he moved.

"That's it, baby girl. You can take me."

"Vicious," she gasped. "Feels so good!"

"*You* feel good, baby. So fuckin' good I can't stand it."

He rolled them so she straddled him, urging her to sit up on him. Once she did, his hands slid up her body to squeeze and knead her breasts before sliding back to her hips. He urged her to move on him, to ride him.

"Move your hips, Lucy. Do that erotic dance you do, but do it on my cock."

Her eyes widened. "Wow," she said. "I must have made quite an impression." She panted as she tried to get a feel for how she could move. She'd never tried this before. Never been on top during sex. Certainly, she'd never experimented with how she could move.

He chuckled. "You have no idea, honey. I've done nothing but think about you since the moment I met you. But, most especially, since I walked in on you dancing in my room. I've never seen anything like the way you move. Fuckin' amazing."

Lucy took over moving on him. She locked gazes with him as she moved her hips in a sensual glide. She let her hands wander up her body to undo her hair as she rode him. She let it fall like a silken cape around her. The long, curly mass brushed her hips. When she arched her back, sliding her hips forward, her hair slid over his thighs as well as her ass.

"Fuck... *fuck*!" Vicious gripped her thighs, his fingers leaving indentions. "The way you move. Fuck!"

She loved the way he looked at her, the way his cock throbbed inside her. He looked at her with something like awe. Sweat sheened his body the harder his cock grew. The muscles of his jaw clenched and released over and over. When he'd swelled almost uncomfortably inside her, he rolled them over once again. This time, he hooked one of her legs over his arm before beginning a hard, driving rhythm.

Lucy gripped Vicious's shoulders. She hooked her free leg around his lean hip and dug her heel into his ass, urging him forward. It felt like she was flying. Her clit throbbed and ached with every scrape of his body against it. The pleasure building and building inside her was unreal. At some point, she heard herself scream, and a burst of intense pleasure shot through her with lightning speed. Her body seized, her breath caught. When was finally able to take a breath, she screamed again. This time, long and loud. Even to herself, it sounded almost agonized. She'd never done that before. Not for any reason, but certainly not from pleasure.

Seconds later, Vicious let out his own hoarse shout, roaring to the ceiling as he emptied himself inside her. She could feel his cock pulsing as his seed spurted. She cursed the condom, getting a perverse thrill in thinking he had come inside her. She knew he hadn't, but in that moment, she'd wanted him to.

When Vicious collapsed on top of her, Lucy let out a contented moan. Her arms tightened around him, pulling him more fully to her. He rested his weight on top of her even as his own arms snaked fully around her.

With a groan, Vicious rolled them to their sides. He kissed her gently, brushing wet curls sticking to her face with sweat.

"You good, baby?"

She giggled. "I don't know. I think so?"

"God, you're beautiful," he said, searching her face for something. "So fuckin' beautiful."

"You're not bad yourself," she said, shyly. She didn't want to get up, but Rycks was probably already with her sister. She needed to talk with him and Mae. Needed to see if going with them was even an option. She wondered if Vicious would really insist she stay. Part of her, the biggest part, wanted him to insist she stay. Wanted him to actually prevent her from going. But she couldn't willingly abandon her sister. It would be far easier to accept if he didn't give her a choice.

"Much as I hate to move," she said, "I need to go talk to Rycks and Mae."

"You're killing me, Lucy," he muttered.

She sighed as she sat up. "I can honestly say that was the best experience of my life, Vicious. But my sister's been through so much. I have to take care of her before I can think about my own life. She wants to go with Rycks so I'm going to talk to him, but she needs me. Her big sister."

"Fine. But I'm going with you."

* * *

There was no way in hell Vicious was letting her leave with Rycks. He didn't care if it was ten minutes across town or ten seconds. Her place was with him. If her sister needed to be with Rycks and Black Reign, that was her choice. He'd learned from Lucy the girl was only seventeen, but from what he knew of their past, Lucy was more of an adult now than most kids in their twenties. She'd lived a hard life. Lucy had tried to shield her younger sister as much as possible, but any woman who could hold her own as a dancer in a strip joint had his respect and deserved a say in her future.

After they dressed, Vicious pulled her into his arms and kissed her. He tried to express with his kiss what he couldn't in words. Did he love her? He didn't know. He'd never loved anyone outside his mother and his brothers, and this was so different it wasn't even the same thing. These last few days with her weren't enough to know if he loved her, but he knew he didn't want to be without her. He'd figure out the rest later.

She pressed her body against his sweetly, wrapping those slender arms around his neck as she kissed him back. He loved the way she responded to him. There was a quiet passion he was dying to play with. Pushing her sexually was something he craved exploring. First, though, he had to secure her with him. He knew this was going to be a fight, but it was one he had to win.

Mae's room was just a couple doors down from theirs, and the second he took Lucy's hand and pulled her into the hall with him, he saw Rycks approach from the opposite end. His heart pounded with fear when he was a man who feared nothing. Would this be the moment when the other man took his woman?

No. That couldn't happen. Hardening his features, he went to meet Rycks head on. The other man looked equally implacable, just as determined as Vicious was.

They stopped just outside Mae's room. When Lucy would have entered, Vicious held her back. She looked up at him questioningly but said nothing.

"I want your personal assurance that, if we let you take Mae, she'll be protected and safe." Vicious stared down the other man, needing to be as intimidating as possible.

Without hesitation, Rycks answered, "On my life, I will protect her. To the fucking death."

Vicious hadn't expected that. He'd expected reassurances. Promises. This was altogether different. Not because of the words. Because Rycks was dead serious. Vicious believed he would absolutely defend Mae with his life. It was the first time he'd seen evidence there might be a chink in the man's armor. He had a weakness. Mae.

"I'll be going with her," Lucy said softly. "I need to know what that means for me."

Everything in Vicious wanted to roar his objection. He wanted to toss her over his shoulder and take her back to their room. He wanted to tie her to his bed where she could never leave him. But he couldn't.

If Mae truly needed Lucy, he couldn't be that mean and selfish. He hoped they could work something out but, much as he would fight, he had to be sure before he did. Mae was in a fragile state. Lucy was her big sister. Vicious knew that, if Mae needed her sister, there was really no option but to let Lucy go.

Until he figured out a way to make her stay.

Rycks's gaze snapped to Lucy. He said nothing, but turned his head to look at Mae huddled under the covers in the bed. "Has she spoken?"

Lucy shook her head. "No. The only time she actually responded to a question was when I asked her if she wanted to go back to Black Reign with you. Please understand me, it's the *only* reason you're here. I don't want her going back to the very people who didn't care enough about her to prevent this in the first place. As I understand it, because your president is in with some bad people Mae got caught in the middle." She let that sink in. "I don't trust any of you with her."

Vicious's heart sank. This wasn't going to be about what Mae wanted or needed. This was about Lucy not trusting Mae's protector. Problem was, he couldn't reassure her, because he didn't blame her. He didn't trust the bastard either.

A flash of pain crossed Rycks's face, and he turned to look at Mae's small form. "In my arrogance," he said, "I thought I had all four of you safe. You all followed the rules, and none of you left the clubhouse. I never thought someone would be so bold as to actually break in. Though there were security measures in place and guards watching the place, I wasn't as serious about it as I should have been. I've since rectified the situation." His gaze swung back to Lucy. "I never make the same mistake twice."

"Four of them?" Vicious asked.

"Yes. Before Lucy and Mae came to us, we had also taken in Serelda and Winter. Too many young women for a club like ours, but someone had to watch over them."

"Are they safe, too?"

"Absolutely. They each have two men who always stay with them. Guards. They have very little privacy, but I've worked hard to make sure they are comfortable with the men with them. Also, I put men on them who understand how fragile they are, and who are able to be gentle with them."

"Sounds like a recipe for disaster to me," Lucy muttered. When he looked at her sharply, she let out a short, exasperated breath. "Oh, come on, Rycks. Gentle? In a club like Black Reign? I doubt any of you know the meaning of the word."

"Since El Diablo took over, he's brought in his own people. There are a few of the original club still there, but most of them... well, they're no longer with us."

Yeah. Vicious just bet they weren't. Bane and Bones both knew firsthand how El Diablo dealt with club members he wanted rid of. It had only been a year since he shot one of his own members in the head during negotiations with Bones.

"Rycks?" Mae voice was soft, but unmistakable. It was the first word the girl had spoken since they'd brought her back. Even Lucy hadn't been able to get her to talk. Now, she made an effort to sit up, but still clutched the covers tightly to her.

The big man turned back to look at her. His features were still hard, but there was a softness in his eyes that surprised the fuck out of Vicious. This man really cared about that girl in some way.

"Hey," he said warmly as he entered the room, slowly approaching her. "There's my girl." When he got to the bed, Mae sucked in a ragged breath before a sob broke free. She shoved the covers down and flung herself into his arms. Once she started, there seemed to be no way to stop the flood of tears. The girl clung to Rycks like he was her only lifeline. Rycks held her, stroking her back up and down with his big hand. He sat with her on the bed, shielding her from Vicious and Lucy as if he knew Mae wouldn't like anyone witnessing her breakdown.

They sat that way for several minutes. Lucy cried softly, and Vicious did his best to comfort her. He wrapped her up in his arms much like Rycks had Mae. To his surprise and immediate gratification, Lucy clung to him. He hated she was hurting, but he wanted her to look to him when she was.

Finally, Mae's sobs turned to little hiccups. Rycks found tissues on the nightstand and dried her tears. He handed her a fresh one so she could blow her nose, then she looked up at him. The sad, lost look on her face tugged at Vicious's heart.

"I thought... I-I thought you got tired of me always hanging around." Her voice was small, so very vulnerable. "We always a-argue and y-you get a-agrivated with me."

"No, baby. Never. I just like watching you get irritated. I like seeing all that fire inside you. Lets me know you can deal with anything if you can deal with me."

"So, you aren't mad at me?"

"I could never be mad at you, Mae. Never."

Lucy watched the pair carefully with narrowed eyes. Vicious could see she still didn't trust Rycks, but wasn't sure what to make of the gentle way he was with her sister. The girl had wrapped her arms around his neck and snuggled into his body like it was her safe haven.

"Mae, honey." Lucy sat on the other side of her, placing a hand on her shoulder. "Baby, look at me." Mae hesitated, but did as her sister asked. Lucy winced when Mae faced her fully. The girl had been beaten pretty badly. One eye was swollen shut, and her face was a mass of bruises in various stages of healing. Vicious hadn't seen the rest of her, but he was certain she looked like that all over. "You know Rycks could come see you every day. Right? You could stay here. I think this club is safer than Black Reign."

Instantly, the girl's eyes filled with tears, and she turned back to Rycks, her arms tightening around him. "Please don't leave me," she begged to Rycks. "I don't want you to go."

"Honey, I'm not leaving you if you don't want me to." He looked up at Lucy. Vicious could see there was going to be a struggle. First Lucy and Rycks, then him and Lucy. He knew the kind of man Rycks was, so Lucy had no hope of keeping Mae from him, and he knew the kind of man he was. He had no hope of keeping Lucy from leaving to be with her sister. Which meant he was fucked.

Chapter Nine

Lucy was becoming desperate. She had absolutely no desire to leave Salvation's Bane and, more importantly, Vicious. It was obvious Mae felt safe with Rycks. She just wasn't certain how much she trusted the big man from Black Reign.

Lucy fought back tears. Until that moment, she hadn't realized how much it would hurt to leave Vicious. Which was ridiculous because they hadn't known each other that long. A couple weeks, if that. Most of that had been questionable. He was gruff and standoffish during the day, but, God, so wonderful at night. So, what should she do?

"Lucy," Rycks said as he rubbed Mae's back over and over. "Mae needs to be with me. You know that." He sounded gentler than he ever had when speaking to her. "I think Vicious needs you with him as much as I need Mae with me. I would never keep her from you, so I'll do something I'd never allow another person. You can come and go at Black Reign as you please." Lucy saw Vicious open his mouth to protest, but Rycks quickly added, "Vicious too. Any time you want to be with her. Day or night. You don't have to call ahead or let us know before you visit. Nothing will be expected of you, and no one will give Vicious shit."

"Really?" What he was telling her was unheard of. "Don't you have to clear that with El Diablo or El Segador? I can't imagine they'd be good with this."

"Already done. After I got back from Mae's rescue, I spoke with them both about this extensively. You can come see Mae whenever you like. Even if one or both of you give us reason to not trust you in our house, you will never be denied access to her." He looked up at Vicious. "If it means anything to you,

Vicious, neither of them hesitated to grant my request. If they had been worried you might betray Reign in any way, they'd never have agreed. No matter what I wanted."

Mae stirred then. "I could come visit you, too," she said softly, finally letting go of Rycks, though not getting down from his lap. She did look up at him questioningly.

"Absolutely," Rycks agreed. "Any time you want, provided Thorn approves the visit."

"If you're waiting for an open invitation from us, you won't get it," Vicious said. "While Mae is always welcome here --"

"I understand and accept that," Rycks said, holding up a hand to stop the lecture. "I was not looking for an open invitation. Wouldn't want one. Much as I respect Thorn and his men, this isn't my home."

There was a moment of silence. Lucy wrung her hands, indecision weighing on her. "It feels like I'm abandoning you, Mae," she said softly. "I never want to be like our mother and father. You're all the family I have left."

"You're not abandoning me, Lucy," Mae said softly.

"We good?" Rycks looked at Lucy instead of Vicious like she would have expected. He wanted her blessing? That was new. Maybe he meant it when he'd said he'd protect her with his life. Did she trust him? She wasn't sure. But Mae did. That was obvious.

"Given all you've been through, Mae, if you're good with this, then I suppose it's only fair that I trust you. The only thing that's important is that you're safe. No one can say you aren't an adult, even if you aren't eighteen yet. You've been through too much to be called a kid. It's your decision, honey."

"I want to go with Rycks." She glanced up at Vicious. "Lucy needs you, though she probably doesn't want to admit it."

"I need her too, Mae."

"I guess we're good, then," Lucy said. "If you hurt her, Rycks. I'll kill you myself."

To her surprise, Rycks gave her a big smile, all the while holding Mae closer. "You'll make a fierce old lady, Lucrecia. Never change."

Rycks stood with Mae in his arms. The men and women of Salvation's Bane were waiting silently in the common room when Rycks entered. Each of them smiled at Mae and wished her well. Vicious and Lucy followed them to the truck Rycks had brought. It was running with the air conditioning going. Lucy was glad to see he wasn't planning on making her ride on the back of a bike. Rycks helped her in and even fastened her seatbelt. He shut the door and went back around to the driver's side.

"Vicious," Rycks said. "Thank you and your club for the work you did to get Mae home. I hope no one was injured too badly."

"We're all good." If Vicious was startled at the thanks, he didn't show it. "Just keep her safe and happy."

"If I don't, I'm sure your woman will take care of it."

"She won't," Vicious said. "But I will."

Rycks nodded before climbing into the truck and pulling out of the driveway.

Lucy had to fight back tears, but she knew it was for the best. "I'm worried," she said softly, not really expecting anyone to hear her.

"Much as I hate to admit it, I trust him in this. He'll keep her safe. It's where she wants to be so she'll be happy." Vicious squeezed her shoulder. "Everything will be fine."

"I hope so. She's my baby sister. I guess it's just hard to let go."

"Come on, honey. Let's go back inside. There's a party tonight, and you could use the distraction." He stopped, looking at her. "Except, no drinking."

Lucy laughed. "Yeah. No drinking."

Then he gave her a wicked grin. "Unless you're up for some wild sex."

Just like that her whole body went hot. Her knees went weak, and had Vicious not had a good hold on her she might have fallen.

"Yeah, I think you like that idea."

* * *

That night, the party was in full swing. Instead of that Godawful metal crap the girls had going on last time, they chose a bunch of classic rock stuff. Skynyrd, Zeppelin, AC/DC, and the Stones along with others blasted through the night. For the first time that day, Lucy seemed relaxed. Vicious proudly paraded her around the party, not letting her out of his sight. If he didn't have an arm around her, he held her fucking hand. Which got him snickers from his brothers when Lucy wasn't looking. He didn't care.

Once again, the party moved to the beach and a bonfire. Vicious noticed Lucy didn't accept any drinks from the girls. She was polite about it, but told them simply, "Learned my lesson the last time." When a couple of the younger guys approached her and Vicious -- casting Vicious wary glances -- and asked if she was going to dance with the other women, Vicious calmly informed them she was not, and that if they asked her again, he'd break their fucking necks. Both had looked crestfallen instead of appropriately scared and expressed their disappointment. Lucy had smothered a grin, no doubt knowing he was put out they were obviously willing to risk his wrath by asking her in the first place.

Vicious supposed he couldn't blame them. She wore a little leather skirt that was barely long enough to cover the cheeks of her ass, displaying her long, lean legs. Her soft white tank was tight, exposing her sexy midriff and the sleek muscles of her abdomen. He wanted to be angry she'd chosen to show everyone what was his, but, the fact was, he loved showing her off. He figured she'd done it for him because he suspected she knew he liked it. Lucy was the most beautiful woman there. And she was his. Was he a bastard for wanting to flaunt that just a little? Probably. Didn't mean he wasn't going to display her if she was willing and excited by it.

He gave her what he hoped was a withering glare, but she just laughed and slid her arms around him. Naturally, he melted.

They stood with his brothers, eating and talking. He'd given her a beer, even followed by whisky but made sure to space them out. She never once balked. She did start to loosen up, her body swaying to the music as if she was just dying to dance.

Obviously, there was no way he was going to even suggest she dance in front of the others. Not only did he know she was opposed to it, but he was a jealous bastard. But he *did* get a positively wicked idea.

Handing her another shot of whisky and another beer, he gradually moved her away from the crowd until they were on the fringe of the party. There he gently backed her against a tree and kissed her thoroughly. She went with him, letting him lead her until they were both panting and she was squirming against him, rocking her hips against his leg.

"Seems my girl is a bit horny." He chuckled. "Was it the music or the alcohol?"

"Mmm, both, maybe. And a healthy dose of you." She sounded dreamy and breathless. "With you so close and your arms nearly always around me, I'm surrounded by your scent."

"I take it you like that." Vicious lowered his mouth to her neck and nibbled. She shivered beneath him, whimpering in her need.

"I love it."

He pulled back and grinned at her. When her eyes widened, he knew she sensed a trap. With good reason.

"Do you trust me, Lucy?"

"You know I do."

"Then turn around for me."

She did, putting her back to his front. Immediately, he slid his hands under her tank, taking in two handfuls of small, firm tit. He pulled and tugged, elongating her nipples until they stood out, stabbing his palms.

"Love your tits, baby. So fuckin' gorgeous."

"Love you playing with them." Unbidden, she pulled her top over her head, dropping it to the ground. Just like he'd hoped she would. They could see the others plainly, but with no outdoor lighting and the fire providing light for the rest of the group, no one could see them. Not that Vicious would care. He'd had sex at parties like this in front of his brothers many times. It was Lucy's comfort alone that concerned him. "Will you suck on them?"

Instead of answering, he spun her around and latched on to one of her small breasts. The whole thing fit in his mouth, and he took great pleasure in sucking until she cried out. Her hands were threaded in his hair, holding him to her. He let go only to take the nipple between his teeth and bite down gently. It was enough to make her yelp, but not enough to cause real pain. When her hips jerked against him, finding his cock and sliding her pussy against it, he repeated the process with the other breast. She moaned loudly, arching her back, offering herself to him so sweetly.

"So fuckin' sweet," he rumbled. "Gonna fuck you in a minute. Right here under the stars beside the sea."

She gasped, her fingers tightening in his hair. Had she balked, he might have managed to make it to his room with her, but now?

"Oh, God! Yes," she whimpered. "Do that, Vicious. Fuck me right here!"

He needed no further encouragement. Kneeling before her, he shoved her skirt up to her waist only to discover she didn't have on panties. "Looks like someone wanted this as much as I did."

"I remembered the last party. The girls didn't seem to mind having sex out in the open, and the breeze feels so good on my skin. I'd hoped…"

"All you gotta do is give me the word, honey. I'm good to fuck you anywhere, anytime, in front of anyone you want."

"That's so dirty!" Her breath came out in gasps, especially when he pushed her folds apart and darted his tongue between them. He found her clit and fluttered it a few times. Not that he needed to. She was soaking wet, her intimate moisture dripping down her thighs.

"Mine," he growled as he sucked her clit. "You ready for my cock? Ready for me to shove it deep? Fuck you hard?"

"Yes! Oh, God, Vicious! Yes!

He stood and spun her around. She spread her legs slightly, and he guided himself to her entrance and heaved upward. He was tall, and she was short. He had to widen his stance to get any leverage, but he managed. He hit her deep in that position, driving her up on her toes, but he held her fast. His hands nearly spanned her tiny waist, which he took great delight in. Every thrust he made was accompanied by a sharp whimper or cry from her. She even dipped her fingers to manipulate her clit and to scissor them around his cock as he fucked her. She might be the death of him. Vicious gripped her hips, pushing a hand against her back until she bent over at the waist while he continued to fuck her.

"Can they see us?" She whimpered. "Can they see you fucking me so hard?"

"Dunno, baby. You want them to? 'Cause I'll walk you over there and give them a show like they've never seen if you want me to. Show them who you're fuckin'. Just say the fuckin' word, baby." He had only meant to add a bit of excitement because he didn't think she was ready for anything else. None of their club members had ol' ladies, but he couldn't imagine them not fucking their women at parties like this if they had them. It was just part of their life. They all loved sex and loved to show dominance in bed. As long as the women didn't mind it, it was a fucking turn-on for most of them.

"Oh, God!" Lucy cried out as she came around him, her little pussy milking him with each contraction. "Vicious!"

He pounded into her, holding himself back, not wanting this to end. Felt too fucking good, and the adrenaline rush was the best high he'd ever had. "Yeah, baby. I think you like that idea. Want me to fuck you in front of my brothers? The club girls? Wanna stake your claim on my cock, baby?"

She looked back at him over her shoulder and bared her teeth. "Don't tempt me."

He kept fucking her, surging even harder into her at her show of temper. "Fuck!" He slammed into her as deep as he could go and held her tightly to him. Gripping her hip with one hand, he pulled her up by her hair until he could wrap that arm around her chest, his mouth by her ear.

"You want them to watch me fuck you? Watch you come on my fuckin' dick? I'll come inside you so fuckin' hard. They'll all see my cum leakin' out of you and know you're mine. Hell, I might even have one of the club girls clean you up... with her tongue."

"Vicious!" This time, she screamed. His woman was a little wanton. An exhibitionist.

"You'd love it, wouldn't you," he whispered harshly in her ear. "Would you let one of the girls eat you out? Clean you up after I pumped you full of cum?" He wasn't sure where that whole bit had come from, but he loved her shocked reaction. It was all about the turn on. Sometimes that meant filthy fantasies never meant to be taken out of the bedroom. So to speak.

"I-I-I don't know! Oh, God!" Her body was now sweating, little beads running down her chest to his arm covering her breasts. "Vicious! Fuck me!"

"I'm gonna. Gonna fuck you so fuckin' hard!" He withdrew and spun her around. She launched herself at him, wrapping her legs around him as he guided himself back inside her. "Unless you tell me not to right now, two things are gonna happen, baby." He waited until she opened her eyes to look at him. All the while, he continued to surge into her, fucking her as hard as he could. "First, I'm gonna call Thorn over here to watch while I fuck you. Need him to bring a quilt for the picnic table anyway. Might as well let you have a fantasy." Her eyes widened, and she swallowed.

"If you trust him, so do I."

Vicious wanted to howl with delight. "That was exactly the right answer, baby. Second, once I've fucked you as hard and as long as I want, I'm gonna come so deep inside your pussy, you'll still be fuckin' drippin' cum tomorrow. You want my cum inside you, baby?"

"Oh, God! More than anything! Please, Vicious!" She moved her hips, trying to go faster and faster. The little wicked movements of her hips were nearly his undoing, but he wanted this. Had the image not become an obsession for him, he'd have gladly and forcefully come right that second. "I'll save the club girls eatin' you out and cleanin' up any of my cum that drips out for another time. But I will see that. I want to see how you like another woman's mouth on your little cunt."

As much as he loved the way she was moving, he wasn't letting her get the best of him. He'd said he was going to do this, and he was. If for no other reason than to prove to her he did what he said he was going to do.

"You good, baby? 'Cause this is happening."

"Do it!" She bit out the command. "Before I lose my nerve."

"You won't, baby. You're like me. You thrive on this shit. I'll protect you and I ain't *ever* sharin' you."

He gave her a hard kiss. "We're gonna have so much fuckin' fun together." He lifted his head and called, "Thorn! Need you over here. Bring a fuckin' blanket with you."

It wasn't long before the Salvation's Bane president, and one of Vicious's oldest and closest friends, came to them, blanket in hand. The closer he got, the harder Vicious got.

"Need you cover that table with the blanket, brother. Want you to watch while I fuck her."

He looked at Vicious sharply before he fisted his hand in Lucy's hair. "Look at me, girl." When she did, her eyes were glazed with lust and adrenaline. "You good with this? Don't want you avoidin' me tomorrow."

"I'm good," she said. "I can give him what he needs." She shook her head slightly. "What we *both* need."

Thorn glanced at Vicious again. When he nodded, Thorn spread the blanket over the picnic table, then stepped back, arms crossed over his massive chest.

Vicious laid her down, spreading her legs wide as he continued to thrust. He grasped her thighs and pulled her closer to him so her ass hung partially off the table. She kept her gaze glued to Vicious as he found his rhythm. Vicious used her thighs for leverage and fucked her. *Hard.* Thorn took up a position above Lucy, sitting at the table so he was right by her head and simply watched the show before him.

"That's it, baby girl," Vicious said. "You look so hot with me fuckin' you. Those little tits bouncin'. My cock looks so big goin' into that little pussy. You like being watched?" They all had their fetishes. Vicious was beginning to think his included having someone watch him fuck his woman, if for no other treason that to prove she was his. Like having someone confirm he was actually fucking her and she was enjoying the hell out of it made her even more his.

"I -- Oh! Yes," she gasped, her breath coming in sharp bursts as Vicious pounded into her. "It's... hot." Her gaze darted to Thorn before returning to him.

"Good. Might fuck you at the party next time. Would you like that? Fuck!" Vicious bit out the last word, his orgasm becoming more and more difficult to fight off.

"I bet that'd be some show." Thorn stroked her hair gently in contrast to Vicious's hard fucking. "Could let a club girl clean you up. Tongue that pretty little pussy until you came again. Vicious might even get off on it. Might come for you both while he watched her eatin' you. Spray your little tits with cum so she'd have to clean that up as well. Would you like that?"

"Vicious!" She screamed as she came, her pussy milking his cock in delicious spasms.

"Lucy!" He bit out her name in a sharp warning. "Don't want to come yet! Feels too fuckin' good! Fuck!" Vicious roared as he came inside her. Never in his life had he come so hard. Stars floated across his vision, and his legs nearly gave out. His hands on her hips cramped, he gripped her so hard. She'd likely have bruises tomorrow, and he'd have to kiss them better, but damn! "*Fuck!*"

He held himself still for several seconds, sweat dripping off his nose and chin to splash lightly on her belly. "Sweet Jesus," he gasped.

"Indeed," Thorn said, his voice decidedly hoarse. "Your woman's hot when she fucks, lucky bastard."

Lucy's gaze darted his way again and she jumped a little. Had she lost herself in the moment so much she'd forgotten they had an audience? Vicious wanted to laugh, but hell, he'd forgotten, too.

"Goddamn," Vicious said. He leaned over her, blanketing her body with his much bigger one and chuckled. "Fuuuuck. Baby, you OK?"

"I am," she said with a smile. "So wonderful."

"Good," Thorn said. "Now, get your asses back to your room. You've created enough of a spectacle of yourselves tonight." He scrubbed a hand over his crotch absently as he turned to leave. "Gonna have to do somethin' 'bout this now. Fuck."

For the first time in a very long time, Vicious was completely contented. Happy even. This one little woman had done that. He chuckled. "If you get to worrying about this, baby, talk to me. I don't want you uncomfortable. I just thought you might like it instead of dancing for the whole club. I know you need it."

She blinked up at him. "I do?" Then she frowned. "I guess I do. I didn't realize that was why I'd always liked dancing. I just never wanted to be a club whore or anything. I definitely never had a guy I trusted enough to have sex with in front of an audience."

"That's all it will ever be, baby. I'll never share, and I'll never want anyone else to touch you during sex. Only reason Thorn was so close was because I trust him like a brother. So, you good?"

The smile that came from Lucy next was glorious. "Best. Date. Ever!"

Vicious laughed as he picked her up and tossed her over his shoulder, naked as the day she was born, before slapping her ass. "Come on, baby girl. Gonna take you to bed. Cause I'm keepin' you forever."

Marteeka Karland

Erotic romance author by night, emergency room tech/clerk by day, Marteeka Karland works really hard to drive everyone in her life completely and totally nuts. She has been creating stories from her warped imagination since she was in the third grade. Her love of writing blossomed throughout her teenage years until it developed into the totally unorthodox and irreverent style her English teachers tried so hard to rid her of.

Marteeka at Changeling: changelingpress.com/marteeka-karland-a-39

Changeling Press E-Books

More Sci-Fi, Fantasy, Paranormal, and BDSM adventures available in e-book format for immediate download at ChangelingPress.com -- Werewolves, Vampires, Dragons, Shapeshifters and more -- Erotic Tales from the edge of your imagination.

What are E-Books?

E-books, or electronic books, are books designed to be read in digital format -- on your desktop or laptop computer, notebook, tablet, Smart Phone, or any electronic e-book reader.

Where can I get Changeling Press E-Books?

Changeling Press e-books are available at ChangelingPress.com, Amazon, Apple Books, Barnes & Noble, and Kobo/Walmart.

ChangelingPress.com

Printed in Great Britain
by Amazon